HOW tía Lola

Saved the Summer

Praise for

HOW Tía Lola
Came to ~~Visit~~ Stay

"Peppered with Spanish words and phrases . . . Julia Alvarez makes the reader as much a part of the 'language' lessons as the characters. This story seamlessly weaves two *culturas* while letting each remain intact, just as Miguel is learning to do with his own life. Like all good stories, this one incorporates a lesson just subtle enough that readers will forget they're being taught, but in the end will understand themselves, and others, a little better, regardless of *la lengua nativa*—the mother tongue. *Simple, bella, un regalo permanente:* simple and beautiful, a gift that will stay."
—*Kirkus Reviews*

★ "The warmth of the individual characters and the simple music of the narrative will appeal to middle-graders. So will the play with language."
—*Booklist,* Starred

"Readers will enjoy the funny situations, identify with the developing relationships and conflicting feelings of the characters, and get a spicy taste of Caribbean culture in the bargain."
—*School Library Journal*

"A delightful book for young adults. Julia Alvarez writes an entertaining short novel that captures young readers' attention and—without being intentionally preachy—she teaches about the importance of having cultural pride."
—*Latina Style*

Turn to the back for a sneak peek at
the next Tía Lola story:
How Tía Lola Ended Up Starting Over

HOW

Saved the Summer

A Yearling Book

This is a work of fiction. Names, characters, places, and incidents either are the product of the author's imagination or are used fictitiously. Any resemblance to actual persons, living or dead, events, or locales is entirely coincidental.

Text copyright © 2011 by Julia Alvarez
Cover art copyright © 2011 by Tatsuro Kiuchi

All rights reserved. Published in the United States by Yearling, an imprint of Random House Children's Books, a division of Random House, Inc., New York. Originally published in hardcover in the United States by Alfred A. Knopf, an imprint of Random House Children's Books, New York, in 2011.

Yearling and the jumping horse design are registered trademarks of Random House, Inc.

Visit us on the Web! randomhouse.com/kids

Educators and librarians, for a variety of teaching tools, visit us at randomhouse.com/teachers

The Library of Congress has cataloged the hardcover edition of this work as follows:
Alvarez, Julia.
How Tía Lola saved the summer / Julia Alvarez. — 1st ed.
p. cm.
Summary: When three girls and their father visit for a week in the summer, it takes Tía Lola to make Miguel forget his unhappiness and embrace the adventures that ensue.
ISBN 978-0-375-86727-9 (trade) — ISBN 978-0-375-96727-6 (lib. bdg.) —
ISBN 978-0-375-89766-5 (ebook)
[1. Great-aunts—Fiction. 2. Dominican Americans—Fiction. 3. Family life—Vermont—Fiction.
4. Vermont—Fiction.] I. Title.
PZ7.A48Hoy 2011
[Fic]—dc22
2010024010

ISBN 978-0-375-86687-6 (pbk.)

Printed in the United States of America

10 9 8 7 6 5 4 3 2 1

First Yearling Edition 2012

Random House Children's Books supports the First Amendment and celebrates the right to read.

For Tía Idalita,
loving and precious tía!
And for Tío Gus
(1928-2009),
whose generosity of spirit,
curiosity, and playfulness
continue to be a blessing.

contents

SCHEDULE for the Week

HOW tía Lola
Saved the Summer

One

saturday

The Arrival of the Swords

Miguel is the first one to see the arrival of the Swords.

He is coming down the stairs when he happens to glance out the landing window. Three girls have just stepped out of the small van and are standing in his driveway, looking up at his house. Their faces show the same dismay as Miguel feels looking down at them.

He should let his mother know. But Miguel wants to delay this female invasion as long as he possibly can. Out of three kids, couldn't at least one of them be a boy?

In the living room, his mother and Tía Lola are finally resting, their feet up on the coffee table. It has been a whirlwind week of cooking, cleaning, fixing up the rooms where Víctor and his three kids will be sleeping. Víctor is

1

the lawyer from New York City who helped Tía Lola get permission to stay in the United States. And he didn't even charge her a penny. So letting his family stay in their big, roomy farmhouse for a week's vacation is the least they can do to return the favor.

Mami notices the look on Miguel's face. "Is something wrong? Remember, Miguel, you promised," she adds before Miguel can even answer her question about what might be wrong.

Miguel and his little sister have promised their mother that they will be good hosts. In fact, when Miguel spotted the girls, he had been moving the last of his things to the little attic room beside Tía Lola's room—so that Víctor and his kids can all be on the same floor. But one thing Miguel is not giving up is his summer fun—even if it is only for one week. He has been so ready for school to be over. Fifth grade wasn't what Miguel (or his grades) would exactly call a piece of cake. And of all weeks to have visitors come! Their first big game of the season is next Saturday. He and his teammates will really have to practice if they expect to beat the Panton Panthers. Meanwhile, Tía Lola has yet to finish their new uniforms. She has been too busy helping Mami get the house ready for their visitors.

"I know I promised." Miguel lets out a sigh. "I gave up my room, didn't I?"

"*Ay,* Miguelito *querido,* you've been such a good sport, my dear Miguelito."

Miguel doesn't like it when his mother gets all mushy: my dear Miguelito this, my dear Miguelito that. Tía Lola has explained that in Spanish you add *"-ito,"* meaning "little," to a name because you love a person a lot. So why call that person "little," especially when you know he does not like being reminded that he is one of the shortest kids in his class?

"Remember, this is the first time those kids have been to Vermont." Mami starts in on all the explanations Miguel has heard before. How when Víctor flew up from the city to represent Tía Lola at her immigration hearing in April, he was impressed by the kindness of the people and the beauty of the state. How he's now thinking of relocating to Vermont, so he's bringing his three kids—twelve, eleven, and five—to look around. Miguel was actually looking forward to their visit, until he found out all these kids were the female kind.

Mami comes over to Miguel, takes his face in her hands, and plants a kiss on his forehead. Miguel has to admit that he has not seen his mother this happy since his parents separated a year and a half ago, a separation that turned into a divorce at the beginning of the year. "Miguel Ángel Guzmán," Mami pronounces his full name, something she does when calling attention to some behavior that needs improvement. But she is smiling fondly at him. "You'll survive. Just remember: some of the best people in this world are girls."

As if on cue, Miguel's little sister comes bounding down the stairs. "They're here! They're here!" She is screaming wildly like the house is on fire. Before Miguel can intercept her, Juanita has lunged past him and flung open the front door. "HI! Guess what? One of you is sleeping in my room, and the other two of you in the guest room, and Víctor in Miguel's room, and Miguel is going up to the attic. . . ."

Miguel can't believe that Juanita is giving everyone their sleeping arrangements before they've even walked in the door. But more incredibly, Mami isn't correcting her. Instead his mother brushes past him, down the front steps, greeting everybody. "Can I help you with that, Victoria? You are Victoria, right?" The tallest one nods. "And you must be Esperanza." She hugs the middle one, who's about eye level with Miguel. "And sweet little Caridad." Mami kneels down and tries to give the littlest one a hug. But Caridad must be super-shy, because she runs off toward the back of the van, where her father is struggling with the door. "Hi, everybody," he calls out. "Be right there."

"And Mami said we can have a campfire and cook s'mores . . . and Tía Lola'll tell us the spookiest stories and we can all make piñatas. . . ." Maybe if Juanita keeps chattering madly, the other two girls will follow their little sister's example, race back to the van, take off, end of story.

But they don't run off. In fact, they seem happier than when they first disembarked. Miguel remembers their sullen faces, glancing up at the farmhouse as if it were a reform school or a haunted house.

"Right, Mami?" Juanita is confirming. "We can do all we want?"

"Within reason," Mami says, then adds, "Whatever the girls want," as if realizing that "within reason" sounds too much like a grown-up's way of saying no in company.

Miguel stands in the mudroom, gazing out at the happy scene. He better call Dean and Sam, his best friends, and see about relocating this critical week of baseball practice to some other place besides his back pasture. Otherwise, the team is bound to get distracted. Mami will insist that Miguel include their guests, even if it's only letting them watch the team practice. Girls screaming and clapping and jumping up and down. There goes his pitching arm!

Suddenly, a hand is squeezing his shoulder. *"No te preocupes, Miguel."* His aunt, Tía Lola, is trying to console him.

He should not worry?! Right! But then, Tía Lola loves everyone, boys and girls, so what would she know about girls getting in the way? "Baseball practice," he mutters. "The game Saturday, our new uniforms, my summer vacation ruined . . ." Miguel sounds delirious. It's as if he's back in Mrs. Prouty's classroom struggling with how to put a sentence together. All year, Miguel's self-confidence has been in the minus numbers, what with all his reading problems, his trying to get used to the idea that his parents are no longer married to each other. But with each passing day of summer vacation, his heart has bounced back, full of happiness and hopefulness and confidence. . . .

"You will have your uniforms, you will win many games, you will have the best summer vacation ever. Tía Lola will make sure." All of this is said in Spanish, which makes Miguel feel doubtful that Tía Lola will be able to work all these wonders in Vermont, where English is the rule.

"But what about the Swords?" he asks. Swords is what Miguel has been calling Víctor's kids all week: *The Swords are coming, the Swords are coming.* It's his little joke, as Víctor's last name, Espada, means "sword."

"I will take care of them," Tía Lola promises just as Juanita, the three girls, their father, and Mami come tromping up the porch steps and into the house. As if that weren't

5

invasion enough, out of nowhere comes a blur of golden fur, heading straight for Miguel. It jumps up, planting two paws on Miguel's shoulders, and gives him a slobbery lick on the face. Not a convincing start to the best summer vacation ever.

"Valentino!" the tallest one scolds in that pretend-stern voice owners use when their pets are doing something adorably wrong. It doesn't fool Miguel for a minute. "Valentino must really love you," she adds, as if this excuses everything.

Miguel wipes his face with his T-shirt. In part, this helps him hide his disgusted expression, which would earn him a scold from his *mami,* and not the pretend kind either. Meanwhile, Valentino lies down penitently at Miguel's feet, his wet mouth open, panting his "pardon me's." Miguel has a sudden vision that makes his heart sink: Valentino chasing after the baseball, getting in the way, delaying the team from honing itself into a well-oiled machine in time for next weekend's big game.

"Let me explain," Víctor is saying to Mami. "Valentino is not staying."

"What do you mean?" Mami sounds as disappointed as if she were being denied her favorite thing in the world: to have Valentino stay in her house for the rest of her life.

"We're taking him to a local kennel—"

"Oh, Papa, do we have to?" the middle one pleads.

"Essie," Víctor says in a tight voice. "Remember our agreement."

The little one, who has been hiding behind her father, is tugging at his pant leg. "What is it, Cari?" But Cari won't

6

speak up, so Víctor bends down to hear her secret. Even before he has straightened himself back up, he is shaking his head. "Absolutely not. A deal's a deal, girls. We're giving our hosts enough trouble with four of us—"

"But it's no trouble," Mami interrupts him. "There's plenty of room in this house for all of you *and* Valentino." She bends down and pulls playfully at Valentino's ears. "Yes, there is. Yes, oh yes," she coos. Talk about mushy. And Valentino is eating it up, wagging his tail, nodding his shaggy head. But all the while, Miguel notices, the dog avoids eye contact with his master, as even a pet must know a deal is a deal.

Víctor is like a dog himself, with a bone. "Our intention was never to bring Valentino along. Sorry, pal, but it's the truth," Víctor apologizes. "We were literally walking out the door when our sitter called. A family emergency. She was flying out that very morning."

"Her mother died in Florida," the middle one offers. "That's where we were going to go, too." A look from her father stops her. She bows her head but keeps muttering under her breath, "Well, we were. Instead we had to come to the middle of nowhere." With her foot, she starts stroking Valentino in a pouty, almost-poking way. The dog doesn't look in the least bit offended. A stroke is a stroke is a stroke when you're a pet, Miguel supposes.

Her middle sister's misbehavior must make little Cari braver, because she speaks up. "Our mother died, too, but in New York. That was a long time ago," she adds because the silence seems to be growing deeper, more awkward. "Right, Papa?"

Víctor runs his hands through his hair. It is thick and black, with silvery strands of gray. He seems at a loss for what to say. Miguel starts to feel sorry for the poor guy. After all, except for Miguel himself, Víctor is the only other male in the room—well, Valentino might qualify. Obviously, Víctor has his hands full with three strong girls. No wonder he wants to move to Vermont. Probably if they stay in the city, that middle one will end up joining a gang like the one that roughed up Miguel during his visit to Brooklyn to see his father last winter break. "We were already late taking off," Víctor continues with his explanation, "so we had a discussion and all agreed"—he looks at each of his daughters pointedly, reminding them—"that rather than try to hunt down a kennel in the city, we'd find one up here in Vermont."

"That way, Valentino can get some fresh air," Victoria adds.

"And exercise," Cari chimes in.

Both are the kind of argument no parent would refute. Miguel can't help being impressed. But then, with a lawyer for a father, these girls have probably learned how to be good arguers.

"We can't accept Valentino staying here," Víctor says with finality, as if he were delivering his closing argument in court.

"No, we can't," Victoria echoes her father, who is flashing an SOS look her way. She is the oldest, and like Miguel, she probably has to set a good example. But Miguel can tell that Victoria would accept Mami's offer in a heartbeat.

"I just don't see why you'd put him in a kennel when

we have plenty of room here," Mami points out. "We've got a big yard and a huge pasture out back."

Miguel can't believe Mami is offering his team's practice field to a dog who'd race around pooping everywhere. He's about to protest, but as if reading his mind, Tía Lola steps forward. "Valentino will stay with me as my personal guest."

Valentino barks his acceptance. Tía Lola claps her hands. As far as they are both concerned, the matter is settled. But Víctor keeps shaking his head like one of those little dashboard dogs with a spring in its neck.

"Vamos a conocernos." Tía Lola changes the subject. She wants to meet everyone.

"I'm Victoria," the oldest says. She is taller than Miguel by several inches. Her long black hair is pinned back with two butterfly barrettes. If Miguel had to write a description of her for English, he'd describe her as pretty. She's not like a model or anything, but her big eyes are shiny and pretty, and her skin is a very pretty soft brown, and her smile lights up her face in a pretty way. Of course, if Miguel wrote all this down, Mrs. Prouty—whom he never has to have as a teacher again, hooray!—would circle the word "pretty" and write in the margins, "Repetitive. Can you think of another adjective, Miguel?"

"I'm Caridad, but everyone calls me Cari," the little one says. She has grown braver and perkier. But then, Tía Lola puts everyone at ease.

"Last but not least . . . tah-rum." The middle one sweeps out one hand. She would have to be the drama queen in the family, the one Miguel will have to attend to, since they're the same age, eleven. "I am the one and only Esperanza!" She takes a goofy bow.

"Victoria, Esperanza, and Caridad, *¡un placer conocerlas!*" Tía Lola beams at the three girls, who must understand Spanish, because they all say back, "A pleasure to meet you, too."

After hugging each girl, Tía Lola announces: "Welcome to Tía Lola's summer camp!"

Summer camp? Miguel doesn't know what on earth his aunt is talking about! And by the looks on their faces, Mami and Juanita don't either. But they do seem delighted to hear that Tía Lola is taking charge.

The middle one's interest is piqued. "You didn't say it was going to be a camp," she confronts her father. "What kind of a camp?" she adds more suspiciously.

"A magical one," Tía Lola says, winking at the one-and-only Esperanza.

"I've never been to a magical camp," little Cari admits, hugging her father's legs tightly, something she does when she is feeling excited or shy.

"What do you say we go upstairs and settle you in?" Tía Lola suggests. "You might want to take a little rest. We have a long night ahead."

"We do?" Victoria's face brightens. This camp is starting to sound like a teenager's idea of fun.

"It won't be scary, will it?" Little Cari has used up her quota of courage for today. After all, she has come as far as she has ever been from home to stay with some new friends Papa made in Vermont.

10

"Not scary at all," Tía Lola assures her. "A nighttime treasure hunt."

"A treasure hunt at night? But how can people even read the clues or see where the treasure's buried?" The middle one scoffs. But she does sound a tiny bit intrigued.

"I have ways to make you see in the dark!" Tía Lola says mysteriously. "Remember, this is a magical camp!" Then, turning to Valentino, she says, "Señor Valentino, let's show the guests to their rooms." And as if Valentino had been living here all his life, he trots up the stairs, leading the way.

Miguel is scratching his head, wondering if Tía Lola can secretly communicate with animals as well as people. Cari and Juanita troop behind Tía Lola and Víctor, who is still shaking his head in disapproval. Victoria and Mami follow.

"Can she work magic?" It's the middle one with the musical name, Esperanza, hanging back, already glued to Miguel.

"We all can," Miguel says before he can stop himself. Some male survival instinct kicking in.

But instead of looking impressed, Esperanza narrows her eyes at him. "So, if you can work magic, will you make my wish come true?"

Miguel shrugs. "Depends." Oh boy, what is he getting himself into?

"Make this week more fun than Disney World."

"Disney World?"

"That's where we were supposed to go for vacation. But then Daddy comes home from some work trip all la-di-da about Vermont."

11

Miguel has to admit that Disney World does sound like a lot more fun than a week in the middle of nowhere—even if a camp has suddenly been thrown into the bargain. But he feels he has to defend the state that's now his home. "Vermont is great," he says, his voice a little less confident than he'd like it to sound.

"So, prove it!" Esperanza says. Then, with a toss of her short, bouncy black hair, she heads up the stairs behind the others.

It's going to take a lot more magic than even Tía Lola can manage to get through this week, Miguel can see that.

Day one of the Swords' visit has begun with a stab to his confident heart.

Two

saturday night

A Nighttime Treasure Hunt

Miguel is upstairs in his temporary quarters, arranging his stuff the way he likes it. Tía Lola has been using this attic room for her sewing projects, but she has moved her machine and materials to one corner so that Miguel can spread out. Since his new room happens to be directly above Juanita's room, Miguel can actually look through the heating vents and see the tops of the girls' heads.

Every single sound comes up through that vent, including Valentino's sighs of reminder that it is a beautiful, if waning, summer day in Vermont. They could all be outside getting some fresh air and exercise.

"So have you been?" Esperanza asks Juanita. She is

trying to build the case that everyone in the world has gone to Disney World.

Juanita lets out a sigh. "Mami keeps saying that maybe the next time we go to the Dominican Republic, where she's from, we can swing by on the way."

"Wow, two cool trips in one!"

"Well, Mami hasn't actually said yes," Juanita explains. She might be feeling bad about getting two special trips when Essie didn't even get one.

"They *never* say yes. It's like parents take a class on how to torture their kids. 'Let's wait and see.' 'I'll think about it.' 'If you get all A's in every subject for the next zillion years, I promise I'll take you to Disney World.' " Esperanza is hamming it up, but then, she has found a receptive audience. Juanita is laughing her head off.

"You're making Papa sound terrible," Cari says in a hurt voice.

"I know," Victoria agrees. "And it's not like Papa promised we'd go to Disney World."

"He was considering it, okay?"

"But considering is different from promising," Victoria points out. "Papa would never break a promise, you know that."

"Then he broke his consideration!" Esperanza seems to like getting the last word in an argument.

As far as Miguel can make out, what happened was that Esperanza kept pestering their father to go to Disney World this summer. After the hundredth time, their father said they would have to wait and see. This was enough of a yes for Esperanza, so that when their father came home from a work trip with the idea of spending a week in Vermont, she was bummed. Especially when he refused to barter that week in Vermont for a week in Disney World later in the summer. A trip to Disney World would involve the cost not just of hotels and meals and rides, but four plane tickets. This was a big expense for a family that might soon be relocating to Vermont, where the father would probably have to take a job that involved a pay cut.

"That's when she went ballistic," Victoria says, shaking her head at her sister's dramatics. "By the way," Victoria adds, changing the subject before they get into an argument over whether Essie asked about Disney World three times or a hundred times, "I really love your room. It's like a tropical wonderland in here."

"Tía Lola helped me," Juanita admits modestly, for a change.

Miguel actually thinks Juanita's room is over the top. Garlands of colorful cut paper crisscross the room. The posts of her bed have been painted to look like palm trees with fronds forming a green canopy in the center. There is also a small purple couch that unfolds into a bed, where Esperanza will be sleeping. That's how the girls have decided it. Meanwhile, Cari and Victoria will be in the guest room, which is connected to Juanita's room by a door. "It's like our very own private suite," Victoria points out.

"Our very own private sweet! Yuuumy!" Cari chimes in.

"A suite, not a sweet." Esperanza doesn't exactly call her little sister "dummy," but her tone of voice suggests that's what she thinks of anyone who doesn't know the difference between an s-w-e-e-t and an s-u-i-t-e. Miguel would never admit it to Esperanza's face, but he himself isn't one hundred percent sure what a suite is. Of course, he does know it's not something you eat.

"Maybe you'll still get to go to Disney World, you think?" Juanita would have to bring up a sore point. But then, very nicely, as even Miguel would agree, Juanita offers to sleep on the fold-out couch and let Esperanza have the splendid bed. That way, even if she isn't in Disney World, Esperanza can at least pretend she's in Florida.

●●●

After an afternoon of settling in, Tía Lola boots everyone out of the house. She has to get the treasure hunt ready. "Don't come back until it's dark," Tía Lola orders, waving goodbye. Since it's summertime, they will all have to entertain themselves until it's almost nine.

"What about Valentino?" Cari asks as they are climbing into the van. They will be eating dinner in a restaurant, so they'll have to leave the dog behind.

"*Valentino es mi asistente,*" Tía Lola announces. Valentino hasn't been in Vermont a full day, and he has already been promoted from guest pet to personal assistant. Lucky dog, all right, Miguel is thinking. He wishes he could stay, but begging off dinner with their guests probably doesn't qualify as being a good host. Besides, they're going to his favorite restaurant, Amigos Café, owned by Rudy, who also happens to be the coach for Miguel's baseball team.

Saturday night, the place is packed. But Rudy has reserved a big round table for their party of seven. "Hey, captain," he greets Miguel, playfully cuffing him on the arm. "Tomorrow we start the heavy lifting."

"So, what exactly starts tomorrow?" Víctor asks after Rudy leaves them to study their menus.

Mami explains that Miguel's baseball team will be having long practice sessions every day through Friday, as they have a big game next Saturday. "Rudy's their coach."

"I'm on the team at my school," Esperanza pipes up. "Papa helps coach when he has time. So, can I play?"

Mami looks unsure, but Miguel is very sure. "This is a boys' team." Miguel can feel his mother's eyes boring a hole into the side of his head.

"That's against the rules! Right, Papa?" Esperanza turns to her lawyer father. "You can't keep girls from playing in Little League."

"We're not a Little League team," Miguel is quick to inform her. Actually, all his teammates *were* in Little League. But now that school is over, he and his friends have decided to stay together as a summer team. Rudy has agreed to coach them.

"That's still discrimination." Esperanza will not quit arguing. "You can't keep someone out of something on account of they're a girl, right, Papa?"

Víctor stands up for Miguel. "But Miguel and his friends already have a team going. They're not recruiting boys or girls. And right now, they have to concentrate on their game so they can win. We'll cook up our own game, just as girls," he adds, winking at his own joke.

17

"And don't forget, there'll be lots to do at Tía Lola's camp," Mami reminds the pouting Essie.

"I know, I know!" Juanita is jumping out of her chair with excitement. "We can be the cheerleaders for the team!"

"Now, there's an idea!" Mami nods enthusiastically.

"*Not* an idea," Miguel says more fiercely than a good host should. "Baseball games don't have cheerleaders."

"That's right," Víctor says, again siding with Miguel. "It'll just distract the players, especially if they're not used to it. After all, we want them to win, don't we?"

Everyone nods vigorously, except Esperanza, whose nod—if there is one—is hidden behind her menu.

As they are getting ready to leave, Rudy comes over to say goodbye. *"Hasta mañana,"* he says, bumping fists with Miguel to confirm that they will be seeing each other tomorrow. Rudy loves any excuse to practice the Spanish that Tía Lola has been teaching him.

Miguel is starting to feel really excited about the upcoming game. Also a little worried. Maybe on account of not having practiced since school let out, the players haven't yet come together as a team. That's why Rudy has decided on long, hard practices daily. By the big game Saturday, the team should be unstoppable! They better be. Miguel sure hopes Tía Lola gets those new uniforms done in time.

"Don't forget to notify the team," Rudy reminds Miguel unnecessarily. It's part of being team captain, setting up practice time and location.

18

Miguel has already called everybody. He has also decided it's too much hassle to try to relocate tomorrow's session. He'll see how it goes. Maybe this camp idea is part of Tía Lola's plan to keep the girls entertained and out of his way. "Only one I've got left to call is Colonel Charlebois," Miguel tells Rudy. Their former landlord is an avid baseball fan and attends every single one of the practices and games. He is also super-generous, paying for the team's equipment, uniform materials, and transportation when they play in another town. That's why they've named the team Charlie's Boys, in his honor.

"He's over there, at his usual post, if you want to tell him now." Rudy nods at an old man dressed in an army uniform, a napkin tucked under his chin. It's like he's going to eat, wipe his mouth, and head for war. Many nights, the colonel eats his dinner here, as he lives by himself in a house he bought in town when the big farmhouse he inherited got to be too much for him.

"Oh, girls, I want you all to meet him," Mami says warmly. Víctor already met the colonel at Tía Lola's hearing back in April. If it weren't for their former landlord's generosity, letting the rent payments be house payments, Miguel's family could never have afforded a big, roomy house on ten acres.

As they head across the room, friends and neighbors say hello, eager to meet the newcomers.

"It's like one big, happy family in this town," Victoria observes.

"It is kind of that way," Mami agrees, slipping her arm around Victoria's waist.

19

●●●

It's almost dark. The sun has gone down but swaths of golden light still stretch across the sky. Víctor drives through town, with Mami acting as tour guide, pointing out landmarks to the Swords. They pass Bridgeport Elementary, all closed up for the summer, the playground looking forlorn with its empty swings and jungle gym.

It gives Miguel a momentary pang of missing school, getting to hang out with his friends all day, racing around during recess. But then he remembers Mrs. Prouty and his difficult year in English class, and the yearning fades.

"That's my school," Juanita points out. "I'm in third. Actually, what am I saying? I'm going into fourth!"

The girls all tell what grade they will be entering in the fall. Esperanza, who just turned eleven, will be in sixth.

"I'm going to be in kindergarten, and it's not going to be scary, right, Victoria?" Cari announces. Her oldest sister reassures her and then adds that she is headed for middle school. "Now, that is scary!" her father remarks.

"How about you, Miguel?" Victoria asks. "Will you be in middle school, too?"

Miguel's confidence begins to revive. "I have to wait another year," he explains.

"You're kidding," she says. "How old are you, anyway?"

When Miguel tells her that he just turned eleven in March, she is incredulous. "I guess it's all the fresh air and exercise of Vermont. You look like you're, I don't know—"

"Twenty!" Cari hollers from her seat in the far back.

Everyone bursts out laughing. Miguel is glad that it is almost dark inside the van. He'd hate for anyone to see how much he wishes he were twenty instead of eleven with one more year of elementary school to go.

●●●

They pull into the driveway. Just ahead, the house is shrouded in darkness. What's more, there's no sign of Valentino. No sign of Tía Lola.

Victoria lets out a surprisingly powerful whistle.

"VALENTINO!" her sisters holler.

Nothing.

"I'm starting to be scared," Cari says in a little voice.

"No, you're not," Victoria reassures her, taking her hand. "Remember, Tía Lola promised it wouldn't be scary."

As if to confirm that, Valentino comes bounding out of the dark woods north of the house. For the second time today, he heads straight for Miguel and leaps up, planting his paws on Miguel's shoulders. That's why Miguel is the first to notice the new accessory. Tía Lola's lucky yellow scarf has been tied around the dog's neck to form a pouch similar to those casks on Saint Bernards' collars. When Miguel undoes the scarf, out tumble five teensy flashlights and a folded-up piece of paper labeled HERE IS YOUR FIRST CLUE. Miguel unfolds the note and reads aloud:

"Turn on your flashlights:
it's darker than you think.

21

You can lead a horse to water,

but you can't make him drink."

"What horse?" Esperanza asks Juanita. "I didn't know you guys had horses."

"I wish." Juanita sighs.

"I don't think it's real horses," Victoria guesses. "It's a saying: 'You can lead a horse to water, but you can't make him drink.' But what does it mean? Hmmm." She can't seem to come up with anything.

"Tía Lola loves sayings," Juanita offers, trying to be helpful. She explains how her school gave Tía Lola a whole piñata full of sayings in English for her to learn over the summer. "Tía Lola probably wants to practice using them. Hey, where are you going?" she calls after Miguel. Her brother has suddenly taken off, the beam of his tiny flashlight dancing wildly on the ground ahead. At his side, Valentino is barking encouragingly.

Miguel is headed for a clearing in the woods where an old well stands. A rusted horseshoe is nailed to one of its posts, probably for good luck, to ensure that the well would never run dry. Inside the bucket, Miguel finds the folded-up piece of paper.

HERE IS YOUR SECOND CLUE, the outside of the note reads. By now the four girls have caught up with him. "You *already* found another one?" Victoria sounds impressed.

"Can I read it? Please, can I?" It's Esperanza, with more eagerness in her voice than she has shown since she arrived in Vermont. Miguel is about to say no, but he remembers his promise to his mother to be a good host. He hands the clue over.

> "I've fallen by the wayside
>
> after so much stony labor.
>
> Remember to repair me:
>
> good fences make good neighbors."

"I know!" Juanita cries out. She's like one of those eager contestants who hit the button before the question is even fully asked. But when everyone asks her, "What?" she admits sheepishly, "Just that it's a saying, too. 'Good fences make good neighbors.' "

Duhhh, Miguel feels like saying. But being a good host means he has to be nice to the other host, too. So he keeps his mouth shut.

"Do you guys have a fence around your property?" Victoria asks.

As a matter of fact, they do. An old, tumbled-down stone wall forms the northern border of the property. There they find the third clue, sitting on top of a boulder, held down by a small stone. This time Victoria reads it. " 'Here is your third clue:

> Now that you are here,
>
> don't wander far from hence!
>
> The grass is always greener
>
> on the other side of the fence.'

"That's easy." Victoria laughs. But after minutes of shining their beams up and down the other side of the stone wall, they are ready to admit defeat. Then, out of the mouths of babes, as Miguel has heard his *mami* say, comes little Cari's clue-cracking question, "Is a fence the same as a wall?"

Miguel is not really sure of the difference. All he knows is that everyone calls the crumbling stone wall a wall or a fence. But where the stone wall stops, a more modern wire fence has been put up. No one ever calls this wire fence a wall. Maybe that is the fence the clue is referring to?

The girls follow him down the length of the stone wall to the wire fence. Sure enough, on the other side, under a patch of grass that probably looks a lot greener in daylight, they find a half-buried plastic bag with a piece of paper inside. As Cari kind of solved the clue with her question, Victoria lets her unfold the note, labeled HERE IS YOUR FOURTH CLUE.

"I'll whisper what it says in your ear, and you can say it out loud, okay?" Victoria offers.

> "Often you have heard this told:
> All that glitters is not gold.
> I should know because I shed
> Blinding radiance from my head."

"I like how it sounds," Cari says after she has repeated what Victoria has whispered in her ear.

"But what does it mean?" Juanita is starting to feel frustrated. She hasn't guessed a single clue.

"Something that glitters but isn't gold. Maybe something silver . . . with a head?" Esperanza is thinking out loud. "A silver statue?" Unfortunately, there are no silver or any other kind of statues on the property. Esperanza gives up. "I wish we'd gotten here a week ago, 'cause then we'd know what to look for."

Miguel can't believe that the middle Sword, who was complaining about being in Vermont at all, now wishes she had come earlier! But Esperanza has a point. After a year and a half, Miguel knows every nook and cranny on their property. Right now his mind is sweeping over all of it: the dirt road, the long driveway, the big front yard, the back pasture, the house, the old shed with its tin roof that flashes when the sun strikes it—

Whoa! Back up there! Isn't flashing sort of like glittering? And isn't a roof the head of a building? And the word "shed" is even used in the clue! Miguel explains his hunch to the girls.

They all agree this is a brilliant guess. Thank goodness, Cari doesn't ask Miguel to explain the difference between flashing and glittering.

At the old shed, Miguel spots the fifth clue, hanging from a nail on the door. But before he can reach it, Juanita snatches at the note, ripping the paper in half. One piece is still in her hand, but the other piece is blown away into the darkness.

"Just read what you can," Victoria suggests after they've

25

searched all around the shed with their flashlights to no avail. "Maybe we can figure it out."

"Something, something . . . 'you will have to find.' And then I think the second line ends with 'mine'?" Juanita hands the torn sheet over to Victoria, who defers to Miguel, who's pretty sure the word is "nine." But that doesn't help much. Find something with nine? Nothing comes to mind. Miguel can't believe his little sister messed up their treasure hunt! What a klutz!

But then, for the third time today, Valentino comes bounding toward Miguel. At least this time he has the courtesy not to jump on Miguel's shoulders. He has something in his mouth, which he pushes into Miguel's hand. It's the lost half-clue! Excellent dog! If Mami ever consents to a new puppy, Miguel is going to put in for a golden-Lab mix just like Valentino.

Miguel and Juanita puzzle the two pieces of paper together. Then Juanita reads:

> "This is the last clue
>
> that you will have to find.
>
> So head for home:
>
> a stitch in time saves nine."

"The last clue is in our house. Hooray! We're almost done!" Juanita cheers.

"We still have to figure out *where* in the house," Esperanza reminds her. "You guys have a humongous house."

"We should have a plan," her older sister agrees. "Otherwise, it'll take all night. So, why don't we work our way

26

down from the attic. That's where Tía Lola's room and your new room are, right, Miguel?"

Something about the way Victoria puts those words together ("the attic," "Tía Lola's room," "your new room") gives Miguel an idea. *A stitch in time saves nine.* A stitch is about sewing . . . could it be that the treasure is hidden in Tía Lola's old sewing room, which is now his temporary bedroom?

Just ahead in the big, shadowy house, a light is shining in his room. At the window, a familiar figure is moving back and forth, as if busily checking on some last-minute details.

"Come on," Miguel calls to the girls. They race across the backyard and into the house and up two flights of stairs to the attic. Taped to Miguel's door, they find a big black *X*. Inside, the room looks like a treasure trove. Piles of golden beads and candy are strewn everywhere as if a huge piñata has just busted open, scattering its contents all over the room. Seven plastic swords dangle from the ceiling. Tía Lola herself is dressed like a pirate, with a black patch over one eye and her own sword in her hand. But the best treasure of all, as far as Miguel is concerned, is the stack of finished, folded, brand-new uniforms on his bed.

Three

sunday

Charity's Challenge

"So, what are we supposed to do with these swords?" Esperanza asks, waving hers dangerously close to a shelf of knickknacks in the dining room.

They are sitting at the breakfast table, having just finished eating the blueberry pancakes Tía Lola cooked up in honor of her guests. The girls are waiting to hear what's in store for their first day at Tía Lola's camp.

Miguel knows his plans: at three this afternoon, his teammates and Rudy are scheduled to come over. That is, if it stops raining.

This morning, Tía Lola woke them up, bright and early, singing "Las Mañanitas," a Spanish wake-up song. In the background, Miguel could hear a soft, soothing patter. . . .

Soothing, that is, until he realized it was the sound of rain pelting the window. Oh no! The first day of practice might have to be canceled. Miguel was so grumpy, he tromped downstairs and didn't say "good morning" to his guests as a good host should, as his mother was quick to remind him.

Everyone was already assembled at the dining-room table. For some reason, they had all carried down their swords, as if they were their meal ticket. Miguel hoped he wasn't going to be sent back up two flights to fetch the one with MICHAEL inscribed on the blade before he could eat his breakfast.

The strange thing about the names on their swords is that they're only approximations, like those monogrammed mugs or key chains on a rack, where you never find your name if it's the slightest bit unusual. Maybe Tía Lola bought these off an English-only sword rack? "Juanita" has become "Joan." Only Linda and Víctor have swords with their same names, although Víctor's doesn't have an accent over the *i*. "Victoria" is "Vicky"; "Esperanza," "Hope"; and Cari's is "Charity," which she isn't sure she likes. Especially after her father explains that charity means giving money to worthy causes, like to feed those sad-eyed, starving kids on TV, who always make Cari feel so sad and scared she has to change the channel.

"Why the swords?" Tía Lola takes up Esperanza's question. "In my camp, every camper gets a sword. Because every camper has something they will conquer during their stay at my camp."

"Even us?" Mami exchanges a look with Víctor. "I mean, aren't we a little old to be campers?"

Tía Lola puts her hands on her hips. "Don't you two know you are only as old as you feel?" She quotes one of the English sayings she has been learning. "And being an adult doesn't mean the fun or the challenges stop."

"You're absolutely right, Tía Lola." Víctor nods thoughtfully. "Sometimes we adults have the biggest hurdles to conquer."

"What exactly is a hurdle?" Cari wants to know.

"A hurdle is like when you are running and there's a fence you have to leap over or a hoop you have to jump through," her father explains.

"So is that what we're going to do today?" Cari asks, frowning as she glances out the window. It looks stormy and thundery and scary outside.

Tía Lola crouches down, eye level with Cari. Valentino gets on his feet, mistakenly thinking Tía Lola has a treat for him. "Sometimes there is something that's hard for us to do, or scary, or a problem we have to solve. And we need all the help we can get. Your sword"—Tía Lola lifts her own sword from where it lies propped in the corner—"your sword will help you conquer whatever stands in your way, so you can become all you really are deep inside."

Cari looks unsure. Conquering problems, becoming who you really are—none of it sounds like much fun. And last night when she was so afraid of the dark room, of the strange noises outside, of the pirates who might return for their treasure in the attic, Victoria promised that camp would be filled with unscary, fun activities.

"How come yours doesn't have a name, Tía Lola?" Victoria wants to know.

It's only now that Miguel notices that Tía Lola's sword is the only one with a blank blade. Probably there's no English version of Lola, though of course, Tía Lola's real name is Dolores. But a sword named Suffering? Get out! No one would buy it.

"There is a reason," Tía Lola says, tilting her sword this way and that. "My sword is reserved for the camper who needs the most help."

"I think we're all going to look pretty silly walking around all week with pretend swords," Esperanza gripes. She would have to see the negative side of things, Miguel thinks. But then, he himself was just thinking the same thing!

Tía Lola stands back up and tucks her sword in her apron strings, grinning her infectious grin. "I do not mind looking silly, especially if it makes other people smile."

"That's right, Essie," her father observes. "And you know, maybe that's something worth conquering, your fear of appearing silly. Especially if having that sword at your side gives you an advantage when you need it."

In the silence that follows this wise pronouncement, Valentino sighs. It's so perfectly timed that everyone bursts out laughing, even Esperanza.

●●●

The girls leave for town right after lunch. Today's rainy-day camp activity is a matinee, to be followed by a "campfire" in the living room tonight. Víctor and Mami drop off Tía Lola and her campers at the movie theater, though at the last minute, Cari changes her mind. The pirate movie sounds too scary, with lots of bloody sword fights. Meanwhile, Miguel stays home, just on the off chance that the rain might stop. Besides, he has already seen this old *Pirates of the Caribbean* movie, not that he ever minds seeing a good film a second time.

Just as the van turns out of the driveway and vanishes, the phone rings. "I'm really sorry, Captain," Rudy tells him. "But I think we better call today a washout. Let's hope for better luck *mañana.*"

Miguel really hopes that the rain'll let up by tomorrow. The team desperately needs to practice playing together. The only piece of good news Miguel can offer is that their uniforms are ready. The team can try them on after practice tomorrow. That way, Tía Lola can fix any that don't fit right.

"You're being a great sport," Rudy compliments him. No doubt, the coach can tell that Miguel is just barely slogging his way through the swamp of disappointment.

When Mami and Víctor and Cari return home, Miguel meets them with such a grim look, they don't have to ask if practice has been canceled.

Soon Mami and Víctor are occupied preparing the living room for tonight's campfire. They laugh and joke as they move furniture around and get a fire ready in the fireplace. Even though it's summer, the rainy day is cool, and what's a campfire without a fire? Miguel and Valentino get displaced so many times, they finally climb up the two flights of stairs to Miguel's room.

As he is going over his baseball cards, Miguel hears a

soft rapping. At first he thinks it's just the rain, but Valentino has gotten up and is standing by the door, his tail wagging. Great! Now Miguel has to deal with a visitor invading his privacy. "Yeah?" he calls out uninvitingly. "Who is it?"

The knob turns. The door slowly opens. Standing there, her left shoulder shyly up to her ear, her sword trailing from her hand, is Cari. "Hi," she says. Her voice is a whisper. "What're you doing?"

Miguel would like to tell her to scram, but she looks so small and scared. "Just going over my baseball cards," he tells her. "Come in if you want."

Cari skips into the room, delighted to be invited. She plops herself down on the bed, lays her sword beside her, then looks all around. "The treasure's all gone."

Miguel doesn't know if he should tell her it was all pretend. Maybe it'd be like telling a little kid there is no Santa Claus. "After we took our share, the pirates came for the rest."

Cari's eyes widen. She reaches for her sword, then decides maybe she doesn't need it. Still, she keeps her hand on it. "The pirates came back to the attic?"

Miguel nods. He's good at solving clues, not thinking up stories and stuff. That's why he was so impressed by Tía Lola's clues last night, especially since they were in rhymes and in English. But Tía Lola confessed that *el* Rudy had helped her write them.

"Aren't you scared to sleep up here?" Cari asks in an awed voice. "What if the pirates get angry that we took their candy and try to hurt you?"

Miguel shrugs. "They don't bother me."

33

"That's because you can work magic like Tía Lola, right?" Cari nods, answering her own question. "Essie told me and Victoria. So when the pirates come, you can just turn them into bully frogs like the ones last night."

Miguel can't help smiling. "Bullfrogs," he corrects her. No wonder Cari was so scared, if she thought the frogs were bullies. "They live down in the pond. And when they make that bull sound, that's just them singing lullabies to their wives and baby tadpoles." He says this last part to reassure her, so she won't be scared of the loud croaking at night. Maybe Miguel's not so bad at making up stuff after all.

"They have wives and babies?" Cari is incredulous. "And they aren't bullies?"

Miguel shakes his head. "They're more scared of you than you are of them."

"They are?"

"Yep! Come on, I'll prove it." Why not? He doesn't have anything better to do than sit around moping about the weather. And it might be fun to splash around at the edge of the vernal pond that never totally dried up this rainy spring. "Are you coming?" he asks, because Cari is still sitting on the bed, cross-legged, her two little hands clutched together as if she were praying.

"But maybe the bullfrogs will jump out and hurt us?"

"They won't hurt you, you'll see." Miguel can tell that Cari is teetering on the edge of fear. But he ignores her hesitation, as if there's no question that Cari is going to follow him into the beautiful, if wet, Vermont countryside. It isn't Disney World, but it has its very own magic.

Miguel heads for the door, Valentino at his heels, eager

for any outing. Behind him, the bedsprings squeak, and next thing he knows, Cari is scurrying to join him. He can't decide if she is being brave by coming or is too scared to stay by herself. As they enter the hallway, she calls out, "Wait!" and races back into the room, grabs her sword where she left it on the bed, and returns to Miguel, breathless with terror and triumph.

●●●

"I'm in shock," Victoria says that night as she pulls her marshmallow from the fire. They are sitting in front of the fireplace campfire, each one with a roasting stick. Cari has just related how she and Miguel caught the half dozen tadpoles that are now swirling around in the Mason jar beside her on the coffee table.

At the table in the dining area, Mami and Victor are finishing up a game of Scrabble. Tía Lola has been tending the fire, adding a log from time to time.

"You did all this brave stuff without us?" Victoria shakes her head in disbelief. "You are really something, Cari baby—"

"I'm not a baby!" Cari protests.

"I mean 'baby' as in hot babe, cool chick," Victoria says, exchanging a high five with her little sister. "And you are, Cari girl! You went up to the attic all by yourself to visit Miguel. You went out in a rainstorm, braving the elements, lightning and thunder—"

"There wasn't any thunder and lightning!" Unlike her middle sister, Cari won't take credit she doesn't deserve.

"That would have been dangerous. Dangerous isn't the same as scary, you know."

Miguel has noticed this before. Cari is very particular about her vocabulary. That must be why she is always asking what words mean. She's probably going to grow up to be an author, maybe an author of dictionaries. Somebody's got to write them.

"Okay, so there wasn't any thunder and lightning, but you went out exploring to a pond full of bullfrogs that you were scared of last night."

"They're more scared of me than I am of them," Cari declares. She demonstrates by patting the Mason jar with her hand. Sure enough, the little tadpoles dart away frantically. "And the big frogs all hopped in the water when they saw us coming, and they stayed hiding and didn't make a sound. Right?" She turns to Miguel. After all, this is too incredible to be believed without the confirmation of a witness. Miguel nods.

"And they aren't bully frogs, they're bullfrogs, because they sound like bulls."

From the table, where their respective parents have one ear cocked to the conversation by the fireplace, Víctor says, "Way to go, Cari. You're going to turn into a Vermont farm girl before the week is over."

"I love Vermont," Cari announces. "It's not scary here. It's more scary in New York."

"One down and two to go," her father remarks to Mami as they pack up their Scrabble game and join the campfire. Miguel must be the only one who overhears the comment, as the girls are busy besting each other's stories

36

of the scariest thing that has happened to them in New York City.

When the girls run out of scary city stories, Víctor starts in on his own story of growing up in New Mexico. His family has lived there since before it was the United States of America, back when it was still part of Mexico. Before the story turns into too much of a history lesson, Victoria asks Mami about the Dominican Republic. What was it like growing up there? One thing leads to another, and soon Mami is plunged into the story of how she lost both her parents in an automobile accident when she was only three. Tía Lola, her mother's younger sister, came from the countryside to take care of her little orphan niece.

The Swords are paying close attention to every word Mami is saying. The story of losing parents is one they can relate to.

"Tía Lola took wonderful care of me," Mami says, misty-eyed. She squeezes her aunt's hand.

Tía Lola squeezes back. "We took care of each other."

"Our mother died three years ago," Victoria says haltingly, as if she were still struggling to believe it.

They all sit in silence, caught up in sad thoughts. Valentino sighs. A log shifts in the fire. In the distance, the croaking of the bullfrogs is relentless, on and on and on. Then, out of nowhere, Cari says, "I'm sorry." But she's not talking to anyone in the room. Her face is right up against the Mason jar on the coffee table. Maybe she's apologizing to the baby tadpoles for scaring them a while ago to prove a point. But then she turns to Miguel and asks if they can go out to the pond again before they go to bed.

"Sure," Miguel says. He's game for a night outing. It'll feel good to walk around after eating so many s'mores.

"I know it stopped raining, but it's going to be awful muddy out there," Víctor cautions, bringing on the hurdles. "It's a chilly night, too. You might catch cold."

"But, Papa . . ." Cari's voice has a teary edge. "The baby tadpoles will be orphans if we don't take them back to their parents."

Who can refuse such a request, especially given the recent topic of their conversation? The world is full of losses, but even so, magic happens: someone steps in to make it better. Tía Lola came to take care of Mami when her parents died. Years later, when their parents separated, she came to visit and stayed to take care of Miguel and Juanita.

Tonight it is Cari, a.k.a. Charity, returning baby tadpoles to their bullfrog parents. Mami and Tía Lola hunt down rain gear, and soon everyone is dressed in old Windbreakers, slickers, garbage-bag ponchos, boots and galoshes and sneakers. They troop outside, Miguel leading the way, followed by Cari, Mason jar in one hand, magical sword in the other.

●●●

Later, on his way to the attic, Miguel swings by to say good night to the girls—Mami's suggestion. But he doesn't mind. He is feeling a lot better, especially after seeing a few stars peeping out from the clouds as they walked back from the pond tonight. It looks like they might have practice tomorrow.

In her room, Cari is crawling into bed. "Night, Miguel!" she calls out, waving her sword before tucking it in beside her.

"What in the world!" Victoria exclaims, her mouth dropping in astonishment.

Cari scrambles out from under the sheets. She hopes there isn't something scary in her bed that she has to be brave about now, too.

"Your sword," Victoria points out, checking both sides of the blade. "There's no name on it anymore." Maybe the letters rubbed off when Cari was trailblazing through the wet field, swooshing at the long grass to be sure there were no porcupines or skunks or snakes or spiders in her way?

Victoria calls Tía Lola from next door, where she is tucking Juanita and Essie into the four-poster bed they have decided to share. "Tía Lola, did you and Cari exchange swords or something?"

"My sword is upstairs in my room," Tía Lola declares. "And your sword never left your side. Isn't that right, Cari?"

Cari nods. The sword has been her constant companion since Tía Lola said it would make the world less scary and help her become the big, brave girl she really is, who will soon be entering kindergarten.

"Now that it's blank, you can put whatever you want on it," Tía Lola says. And just like that, she pulls a marker out of her pocket so that Cari can write her real name in big, bold letters across the magic blade.

39

monday

Víctor, the Victor

Monday dawns with a bright sun, flashing off the shed's tin roof. By afternoon, the pasture will definitely be dry and ready for baseball practice. Miguel is feeling on top of the world, as if he really can work magic.

At breakfast, Víctor offers to help Miguel get the playing field ready, gathering the branches and twigs the rain brought down. Mami is relieved, as this will keep Víctor entertained until she gets home. Summer school is in full session, and though Mami is taking off a few days after July 4, she has to put in some hours today at the office. The girls will be fine in Tía Lola's excellent care. Today, in fact, Tía Lola is running a sort of summer-camp spa, doing the girls' nails, giving them pedicures, and curling their hair, before they go to town to shop. A girly-girl day. Only Esperanza seems less than delighted with the prospect.

After breakfast, Miguel and Víctor head for the back pasture. They stop at the shed to deposit the baseball equipment they brought along. Before he stacks the last bat in the corner, Víctor takes a few swings. "Brings it all back," he says dreamily.

"Brings what back?" Miguel is curious. They've been talking baseball nonstop: scores, players, teams.

"Oh, you know, being your age, having big dreams," Víctor reminisces. "I wanted to be a major leaguer bigtime. We didn't really have much of a team to root for in New Mexico, but I watched all the games I could on TV. Even organized my own team. We got pretty good. My coach came out to talk with my *familia*."

"Cool," Miguel says, taking a second look at Víctor. It is surprising when someone your parents' age turns out to have dreamed your dreams. "So what happened? Did you go for it or what?"

Víctor sighs, a sigh so deep and sad, it takes Miguel's breath away just hearing it. "I was the oldest of seven. Always had to help out. Still, I played all through high school, college, whenever I could. Law school was tough, though. Worked a night shift and weekends to pay my way. Then I got married, along came the kids, my wife got sick. . . ." Víctor's voice drops off.

It always makes Miguel sad when adults start talking about how they've had to give up something they really love in order to take on their responsibilities. Doesn't give growing up a good name at all. But then, Miguel can also

41

see that it hasn't exactly been Víctor's choice to have his wife die and stuff. Just as it hasn't been Miguel's choice to have his parents divorce.

"But hey, I ended up with three great kids," Víctor adds, as if realizing he's gotten them both knee-deep in some sad memories. "And I'll tell you, that Essie, she's a ballplayer. Quite the mean pitching arm. It's been kind of nice, getting back into baseball by helping coach her team."

"So you really do coach?" Miguel wasn't going to take Essie's word for it.

"Absolutely! In fact," Víctor adds, looking over his shoulder like some cleanup supervisor is watching them, "how about we work on a few pitches before picking up?"

The morning ticks away. It's almost noon when man and boy scramble to finish the cleanup. By the time they head to the house for lunch, Miguel has learned to throw a wicked curveball. He has also had a surprisingly good time.

Miguel hopes that his *papi* will understand that Víctor isn't a substitute father or anything. Miguel would much rather hang out with his own father, but then again, Papi has never shown an interest in anything but *watching* his son play baseball.

●●●

As they come down for lunch, the girls sure look and smell different. Their hair is curled, their nails are painted pearly white and pink, their lips are shiny with lip gloss. The only one who looks normal is Essie, who hasn't changed a bit.

42

Víctor goes over the afternoon plans. After lunch, he'll drop Tía Lola and the girls off in town. But how will they get back? "Maybe it makes more sense if I just come along?"

Victoria does not want her father hanging out with them while they shop. That would ruin everything. Papa does not approve of what he calls "consumer madness," unless it's taking place in a bookstore in the history or sports section. "Linda said we could catch a ride with her after work."

"Either that or we can just hitchhike," Essie says airily. It's as if she's purposely baiting her father.

It works. Víctor's face is a mask of concern. "You must never ever—"

"Get in a car with a stranger," the Swords chorus, giving themselves high fives all around and laughing hysterically.

Víctor waits until the laughter dies down. Then he makes his daughters promise they will never ever get into a vehicle with a stranger.

"You know that rules out ambulances, Papa," Victoria says, a twinkle in her eye. It's nice to see her being a little naughty, as she's always so well-behaved. "Our poor papa. You're going to get even more gray hairs, worrying about us." Victoria gives him a peck on the cheek, just so he doesn't start worrying about getting old and dying.

Miguel has noticed that Víctor sure is a big worrywart when it comes to his daughters. But if he keeps worrying, he'll never even let himself coach baseball. He'll worry about coming home too late after practice or being gone for away games. If not that, he'll worry about getting hit by a ball and killed and making the girls orphans. Miguel wishes he could say all this to Víctor, but as he himself knows, all the advice in the world doesn't help until you are ready to change from deep inside.

"By the way, you girls all look like you had a fine time getting makeovers at Tía Lola's spa," their father says. He looks relieved to be changing the subject.

"I did *not* get made over," Essie defends herself. It's as if her father has accused her of a crime. "I was out front practicing." Tía Lola found her an old bat Miguel had left behind in the attic, as well as a bag of old balls. Essie has been tossing them up in the air and hitting them against the side of the house. "Not near any windows," she is quick to say, before her father, who worries about such things, can remind her.

"Oh, Essie, I haven't forgotten," her father says apologetically. Of course, he'll keep his promise to play ball with the girls. Not that he has any other takers besides her. "I'll tell you what. Let me drive the others into town. Then you and I can have our own practice. We'll stay in the front of the house, out of the team's way," he adds, to reassure Miguel. "Sound all right to you, Captain?"

Miguel hesitates. He would actually prefer if *all* the girls were gone, especially the middle Sword. But even without Mami around to remind him, he knows he would be a bad host to say so. Besides, he totally trusts Víctor to keep his promise of steering clear of the team's practice. Not that he would mind some tips from Víctor. Just from their session this morning, Miguel can tell that Víctor has that special baseball intelligence that could help the team win their game Saturday.

●●●

Víctor and Essie are already at it by the time Miguel's teammates begin arriving. Soon a small crowd has gathered, watching the pair. Essie looks like a pro—every pitch under perfect control. Her father calls out pointers.

"Who's that?" his teammates keep asking Miguel.

"A friend of my mom. That lawyer from New York City who helped Tía Lola."

"No, not him. The other one. The girl."

"She's just his daughter."

Just nothing, their expressions seem to say. We know a fireballer when we see one. "Wish I could play like that," Patrick says wistfully. Being the team's smallest, weakest player is no fun. "Maybe she'll practice with me, you think?"

Miguel now wishes he had made more of a fuss about Essie staying behind with her father. But how was he supposed to know she'd be such a good ballplayer, making him and his teammates feel average?

Next pitch is a fastball that should get a speeding ticket. Rudy has just pulled up in his pickup with Dean and Dean's older brother, Owen, who's helping coach the team. Rudy has been having a hard time recently keeping up with the kids. Must be getting old, or maybe he's just too busy with the café to summon the extra steam. "Way to go!" he calls out to Essie.

45

Víctor and Essie come over to say hello. One thing leads to another, and Rudy finds out that Víctor has been coaching his daughter's team in the city. "Anytime you guys want to join us," Rudy invites them, making Miguel's self-confidence take another nosedive. But just as he thought, Víctor remembers his promise. "Thanks, but I know the team really has to stay focused, no distractions. And hey, we're having a great time ourselves, isn't that so, Essie?"

But Essie has heard an offer she can't refuse. What's more, she herself never made a promise to stay out of Miguel's way. "I know I can't play or anything," she tells Rudy, ignoring her father's widening eyes, "but maybe I can come watch?"

"Anytime," Rudy says, not noticing the very slight shake of the head the girl's father makes in Miguel's direction.

●●●

Maybe Miguel was distracted with the idea that Essie would wreck everything, or maybe he shouldn't have left his good-luck sword back at the house. Not that he could have played ball while carting around a plastic sword almost as big as a bat. But maybe having the sword close by would have avoided what happened. Somehow, as he was winding up a pitch, he tripped and twisted his ankle.

Víctor must have heard the yelps of pain and raced down, because he's the one who carries Miguel off the field. After conferring with Rudy, Víctor decides Miguel should be seen in the emergency room to rule out a fracture.

46

"Today is your lucky day," the emergency-room doctor tells Miguel after peering at the X ray on the lit-up panel. "There's no evidence of a fracture. But you will need to stay off the foot for at least a week."

Víctor, who has been pacing the length of the narrow examining room, stops in his tracks. "A week!" he exclaims at the same exact time as Miguel.

"Sorry, guys," the doctor apologizes to both, as the man seems just as upset as the boy. "But you don't want to hurt the ankle so you can't play for the rest of the summer, now do you?"

Miguel can't stand it when adults ask such ridiculous questions. What's he supposed to answer? Oh, yes, sir. I would very much like to hurt my ankle and not play baseball all summer. "But what if I take really, really good care of it for a day and it feels totally cured? Can I play then?"

The doctor is shaking his head. "It'll take more than a day, sorry."

"But there's got to be something you can do," Miguel pleads. He is ready to endure anything, even a whole bunch of needles or an operation, just as long as he can play ball by Saturday.

"Listen, here," the doctor says, growing a little testy. "My professional opinion is you need to rest it for a week. That's all I can offer as a doctor. Short of that, I'd be dabbling in miracles."

Víctor and Miguel exchange a look. A lightbulb has gone on in both their heads. It just so happens they know someone who might be able to help Miguel get miraculously better right away.

47

●●●

Back at the house, Mami and Tía Lola and the girls have all heard the news from Essie. Mami is so worried, she's ready to drive to the hospital, but just then the van turns into the driveway. There is quite a fuss as Víctor carries Miguel up the front steps, Mami asking about fractures, the girls clutching their throats dramatically like Miguel's some wounded soldier returning from the war.

After practice, the team streams in, wanting news of their injured captain. They're also supposed to try on their uniforms, but they feel a little sheepish asking about it, given the bad news that Miguel might not be able to play in Saturday's game.

"Hey, team, I want you all up in my room *now* to try on your uniforms," Miguel orders, surprising even himself. His team's morale shouldn't be brought down by his bad luck. For a moment, he feels an odd, grown-up sensation, putting the happiness of others before his own.

Víctor insists on carrying Miguel up the two flights, despite his protests. He doesn't want to look like a baby in front of his teammates. "Just want to protect that ankle until we talk to Tía Lola," Víctor explains in a whisper.

Miguel is grateful that Víctor has not mentioned what the doctor said about staying off that foot for a week to his mother. That's all Mami needs to hear. Then, even if a miracle were to happen, his ankle magically healed, Mami would not let Miguel stand on that foot until a week—to the minute—was up. But Miguel isn't sure how long Víctor will keep his mouth shut, given that he is such a worrywart

48

himself. Besides, loyalty among parents has got to be stronger than loyalty among baseball fans.

Tía Lola has been in and out of Miguel's room, assessing which uniforms need adjustments. When the last team member leaves, Víctor calls her back in and closes the door. "We've got something to discuss with you, Tía Lola." He is nervously pacing the length of the small room. Miguel is feeling equally nervous, sitting on his bed, his bruised ankle propped on a pillow, his good foot jiggling like crazy.

"We know that you have special abilities." Víctor stops short because Tía Lola is shaking her head, denying this fact. Víctor flashes Miguel the same SOS look he sometimes gives Victoria when he needs her help managing some temper tantrum or enforcing some rule. But Miguel can't think of how to approach Tía Lola either. How do you ask somebody to work a miracle?

"Isn't it a fact," Víctor continues when Miguel doesn't speak up, "that the swords you gave us have, by your own account, the magical ability to help us face a special challenge?" Víctor is sounding too much like a lawyer, taking a long time to say something simple. At this speed, Mami will soon be upstairs wanting to know why they haven't come back downstairs.

"The doctor said I had to stay off my foot for a week unless there's a miracle," Miguel blurts out.

"I see," Tía Lola says, letting herself down into the rocking chair with one of the uniforms she needs to fix. She looks carefully at Miguel and then Víctor, as if she can see way down to the bottom of each one. "You want me to work a miracle?"

49

Víctor lets out an embarrassed laugh. After all, he's a grown-up, a professional man, a parent—all the requirements for not believing in miracles and magic. And for most of his adult life, that's what he has been, a hardworking, sensible citizen. But right now he needs his life to go another way. He wants this boy to get to play the game that he, Víctor, had to give up. "I guess that is what I'm asking for." He shakes his head, as if he can't believe what he hears himself saying.

Miguel is nodding. "Me too, Tía Lola, please! You know how much this game means to me."

Tía Lola holds up a hand to stop them. "I think I might have given you both the wrong impression. The swords are to help you. You see, we have to work our own miracles."

This does not sound good. Miguel bows his head to hide his tears. Not only has he turned into a lame baseball player, but he's become a crybaby as well.

But Víctor won't give up. "Okay, fair enough. We'll work our own miracle. Right, Miguel? First, we're going to stay off the foot until tomorrow night. And since we don't want to sound the alarm with crutches, you're going to have to let me carry you everywhere."

Miguel hates to tell Víctor: if using crutches might set off Mami's worry alarm, what about being carried everywhere? But Víctor is sounding like a kid determined to believe in magic.

"So where are your swords?" Tía Lola asks out of the blue.

Víctor has to think a moment. "I believe I left mine in my room."

Tía Lola nods at her nephew. "And yours, Miguel?"

He sniffles a little, wipes his nose, gets his voice back under control. "I left mine in the mudroom." He doesn't have to explain, because she knows why. He didn't want to look silly in front of the guys.

"You'll need your swords," Tía Lola tells them. So maybe she *is* going to try to help work some magic after all? She did promise to use her sword to help the person who needed it most. And Miguel really needs help if a miracle is going to trump modern medicine.

"I'll go get them," Víctor offers. "Don't you worry, captain. You're going to hit them right out of the ballpark."

They hear him hurrying down the hall at a fast clip, Miguel's mother intercepting him on the stairs, her worried questions, his don't-you-worry answers, their footsteps descending together. A long, thoughtful silence fills the room. Finally Tía Lola says, "You've helped do a very good thing, Miguel, you know that?"

Miguel is puzzled. All he can think of is the very bad thing he has done to himself, twisting his ankle, possibly taking himself out of their first big game.

Tía Lola's nods are in sync with the rocking of her chair. "Oh yes, you did. Víctor has been a workhorse since he was a little older than you. Shouldering all kinds of responsibilities. But today, with you, he's found that little part of himself he left behind."

"You mean the part that wanted to play baseball?"

Tía Lola considers for a moment. "The part of him that's a kid who believes in magic and miracles, instead of worrying all the time that the worst is going to happen."

That's the way Miguel is feeling right now. Maybe he and Víctor have exchanged personalities. From now on, Miguel will be super-cautious and serious and no fun to be around.

"Don't lose that part of yourself," Tía Lola says, as if reading his thoughts. Her tone is gentle but her gaze is fierce. "Because if you do, you will have lost the game, the big one called life."

All of this sounds a little too profound, like the deep end of the pool of his mind that Miguel dives into only when he's in church or taking an exam. "I just want to be able to play ball, Tía Lola," he says, trying to keep it simple. "And I want to play this Saturday, if at all possible." He adds this last part because maybe it won't be the end of the world if he can't play their first big game. Maybe it would be worse if he gave up altogether just because this once he might not get what he wants. If he turned into an adult talking to a kid about what might have happened. Just like Víctor this morning on their way to the field for cleanup.

As if summoned by that thought, Víctor comes in the door, carrying both swords. "Here you go, *Michael*," he jokes, handing Miguel his sword.

"And now, Tía Lola, I want the truth, the whole truth, and nothing but the truth." Víctor is using his lawyer language again, but this time it's with a smile on his face. "Can you tell me who did this?" He holds out his sword, pointing to where a little black accent mark has been inserted over the *i* in "Víctor."

Tía Lola's eyebrows lift like two accent marks over her

eyes. *"No sé."* She has no idea. As she has already told them, they have to work their own miracles.

"I guess I'm turning into a miracle worker, then." Víctor laughs. "So what do you say, Captain, we plaaaaaaaaaay ball!" He swings his sword at an imaginary ball and then puts his hand above his eyes as if he's trying to make out a distant object.

The guy has gone batty, Miguel thinks. But he can't help laughing; there is something very winning about a person who believes in magic.

Five

tuesday

Juanita's Especially Special Fourth of July

Juanita sits on the back steps, her elbows on her knees, her face in her hands. She lets out a long, sad sigh. She was so excited about the Swords coming just at that point in the summer when she would be starting to miss her friends from school. Then she was so excited when Tía Lola thought up a summer camp with movies and makeovers and s'mores. But now, on the fourth day of the girls' visit, things aren't going as planned.

For one thing, the summer camp idea seems to have fallen apart. Essie and Victoria are down in the pasture with their father and Miguel and the team. Essie has been asked to step in for the day while Miguel's ankle heals. Meanwhile, Victoria has suddenly discovered a keen interest in

54

baseball. That leaves Cari for Juanita to play with. Juanita knows she promised Mami, but a baby five-year-old is not the best company for a nine-year-old headed for fourth grade to hostess.

Juanita has done her part. She read Cari her old picture book about tadpoles becoming frogs three whole times. She tried to be patient as Cari tagged along, asking questions, wanting to join in with whatever Juanita was doing. Could she also draw a flag with Juanita's markers? Could she also help dress the dolls for a Fourth of July tea party? Could she try on Juanita's tutu and pretend to be a ballerina fairy godmother? Finally, Juanita had had it.

"Can't you go play with someone your own age?" she snapped at the little girl unhelpfully, as there's no other five-year-old in the house. "You're being a pest!"

Cari got all blinky-eyed and red-faced. Head bowed, she walked slowly downstairs to the kitchen, where Mami and Tía Lola were cooking up a storm. The odd thing, and something that Juanita wasn't counting on, was that her outburst didn't make her feel any better. But she couldn't help herself. Juanita wants something fun to do and someone her age or older to do it with.

Another thing she wasn't counting on is how she is no longer the best at anything. Before the Swords came, Juanita was the best at reading, the best at Spanish, the best at using her imagination. In other words, with only one other sibling, she was the best at least half the time, actually more. But now, with three additional kids around, Juanita hasn't been able to distinguish herself. During the treasure hunt, it was Miguel and Victoria guessing every clue. All Juanita did was tear up a crucial clue that would have ruined the whole hunt if Valentino hadn't come to the rescue. Even a dog has bested her!

Juanita isn't so sure anymore that she wants the Swords sticking around past Sunday, something she has heard Mami and Víctor murmuring about. Otherwise, she'll never again be the best at something.

As she contemplates this grim prospect, Juanita senses someone beside her. It's Tía Lola, with that look in her eye. She knows something is wrong before you even tell her. *"¿Qué pasa, calabaza?"* she asks. What's wrong, *calabaza*? Juanita usually understands Tía Lola's Spanish. But today, she hasn't a clue what her aunt is calling her.

Tía Lola points to the pumpkin vines out in the garden. "The *calabaza* is what grows on that vine."

Great! Now Juanita is a vegetable, which, come to think of it, is exactly how she feels.

Inside the house Juanita can hear her mother finishing up preparations for today's Fourth of July barbecue. Cari is helping her count out all the silverware. They were not going to have a big party, but after Miguel got hurt yesterday, Mami talked to all the parents as they were picking up his teammates. A whole bunch agreed to pool together and have a potluck Fourth of July barbecue. Six families will be coming over later this afternoon, as well as Colonel Charlebois; Stargazer, Mami's friend with the fun shop in town; and Rudy and Woody, as the café is closed for the holiday. The team also decided to hold a pre-party practice after all. Why not? While the weather holds.

So, it's turning out to be a special Fourth of July after

all. But Juanita feels so unspecial that what she notices is what won't be special about it. No fireworks. They've been canceled due to the rain prediction. What's a Fourth of July celebration without fireworks?

Tía Lola sits by quietly, keeping her niece company, not nagging her to say what's wrong. From the back steps, they look out at the magnificent, thriving garden. This year, in honor of her application to be a resident of this country, Tía Lola planted the garden in the shape of the United States. "I'm going to go weed in Florida," she'll say. Or, "I'll go pick asparagus in Oregon and drop by Minnesota for radishes on the way back." Anyone hearing her would think Tía Lola was actually headed for those states to harvest their dinner.

"Everyone has something to do except me." Juanita finally speaks up. She was feeling too cranky and upset to talk to anybody, even Tía Lola, but suddenly the words are spilling out. "I can't do anything really special anymore," she confesses. This must be the way her brother feels when Juanita gets praised for being the best reader, the best student, the best in learning Spanish.

Tía Lola puts her arm around Juanita's shoulders. "*You* are especial, and that makes everything you do especial."

Juanita has to smile. She has corrected Tía Lola countless times, but Tía Lola keeps forgetting and saying "especial" instead of "special" because that's how you'd say it in Spanish. Either way, Juanita would like very much to believe her aunt. But she has a long list of all the things she has done within recent memory that are not special. "Even my s'more fell into the fire."

"That's because you were trying to help Cari with hers, and that was especial," Tía Lola reminds her. Juanita used her roasting stick to lift Cari's out of the fire, and her own marshmallow fell off. But instead of feeling special about her kindness, Juanita feels bad all over again about hurting little Cari's feelings earlier today.

"And look at your masterpiece." Tía Lola gestures with her arm. Flanking her United States vegetable garden is a sea of flowers, all Juanita's, as she asked to be the one in charge of the flowers this year. And what a sight! Her lilies are up, her bleeding hearts, her sweet peas, her zinnias, her morning glories, her marigolds, her nasturtiums, her periwinkles, her ager-somethings. Juanita did go a little overboard. But then, that's easy to do, ordering from a seed catalog in the middle of winter.

"But what good is it, Tía Lola, when no one even notices it?" There's been so much excitement about their guests' arrival, Cari's brave deeds, Miguel's accident, no one has paid attention to her work of art. Not even Juanita.

"*Ay*, but lots of guests are coming to the barbecue," Tía Lola reminds her. "Wait till they see your garden! They will love it. But first, *you* have to love it, and that means we have work to do. Where is your sword?" Tía Lola is on her feet, looking her niece over as if Juanita is missing a critical part of her own body.

Juanita shrugs. "My room, I guess." She doesn't know why she is pretending she doesn't know where her sword is. She left it lying on her window seat, where she had tried to curl up with a good book. But as much as Juanita loves reading, she couldn't take her mind off how mean she'd been to Cari.

"Why don't you go find it and meet me down here in a few minutes."

What is Tía Lola up to? From the kitchen window behind them, Juanita hears Mami praising Cari for the fabulous job she has done counting out all the silverware. Far off, Miguel's teammates are cheering. Everywhere people are being singled out for doing special things, while Juanita sits on a back stoop being ignored by the whole world. She gets up slowly, with a tired sigh. She hates to tell her aunt, but she doesn't really believe Tía Lola can help her feel special this Fourth of July.

●●●

The funny thing about feeling sorry for yourself is that once you're busy doing something you really love, you kind of forget to remember yourself. Juanita is so caught up in her garden, harvesting flowers while Tía Lola readies several dozen Dixie cups, that she doesn't notice when the shouts and calls have stopped in the back pasture, the team streams by, the cars come down the driveway as the guests start to arrive.

Her sword has been so handy. The plastic edge is suddenly sharp enough to use for cutting stems, but not too sharp that she might cut herself. The letters rub off the blade as she works. Who cares? Joan isn't really her name, after all. At one point, when she's standing very still, a pale yellow butterfly lands right on her bee balm and then on her arm. Juanita had forgotten how much she loves growing flowers!

As they work, Tía Lola and Juanita talk to the flowers, thanking them, explaining why they are cutting some and not others. Tía Lola has told Juanita that this is very important, since all plants, and especially flowers, like it when you pay attention to them. Just like me, Juanita can't help thinking.

"They look so pretty," Juanita says, admiring the tray full of Dixie cups, each one filled with red and blue and white flowers. The center of each table will be lined with these patriotic bouquets. What a wonderful surprise for the Fourth of July! Once everyone has eaten, Juanita will come down the stairs in the long white robe from the angel costume Tía Lola made her for *carnaval*. Stargazer is bringing the hat Juanita remembers admiring in the window of her shop. Juanita can't wait to see everyone's face light up at this especially special surprise Tía Lola has thought up.

●●●

Almost as if drawn by the promise of a party, the clouds roll in. The random drops turn into a serious patter, and then throwing caution to the wind, the rain pours down. Good thing those fireworks got canceled.

Anticipating bad weather, Mami and Víctor set up the folding tables in the sunporch, jokingly calling it the rain porch. Out back, in their raincoats, Rudy and Woody are grilling hamburgers and hot dogs. Meanwhile, the dining-room table is piled with enough food to feed a whole village—fried chicken and potato salad, deviled eggs and cheese sticks, *pastelitos* and rice and beans, and every imaginable kind of pie.

Everyone is in high spirits, exchanging stories of their summer so far. Most of the talk is about gardens: what's doing well with this rain, what isn't. "Yours is amazing!" people exclaim when they look out at the backyard. "Would you take a look at those flowers! And those darling centerpieces!" Whether or not they know it's her doing, Juanita's heart swells. People are loving something she helped create.

"You're going to have to come over to my garden," people remark after Tía Lola tells everyone who did the flowers. At this rate, Juanita will be booked all summer as a flower-garden consultant.

"My brother and Tía Lola did the vegetables," Juanita admits, humbled by all this recognition. She looks around for Miguel and spots him sitting on the couch, his leg propped up on the coffee table, obeying orders from "Dr. Víctor" to stay off his foot. Maybe it's the sword tucked under her arm, but suddenly, it's as if Juanita has X-ray vision or something. She can tell how tough a day it has been for Miguel, not being able to play, having to watch Essie pitch. And yet he's been such a good sport. Better than she, Juanita, could ever hope to be. Juanita feels a sudden gush of love for her wonderful, sweet, selfless brother. And, surprisingly, she doesn't feel any less special just because she can see Miguel is also special.

"You're the best brother in the world!" Juanita exclaims,

plopping down beside him. She is about to throw her arms around him, but she can see him flinching, not wanting to be embarrassed in front of his friends. "You don't believe me?" she asks because he looks wary. Juanita has been running in and out of the room, up and down the stairs with Tía Lola—always a sure sign she is up to something.

"Okay, so I'm the world's greatest bro. How come you just realized it?"

"Having the Swords here made me realize how lucky I am I've got a brother, you know?"

Her brother frowns, pretending annoyance, but she can see he is gratified by this admission. Then a mischievous smile hooks up the corners of his lips. "Well, I can tell you that having them around has made me realize how lucky I am I have only one sister."

Juanita gives him a peck on the cheek, real quick so no one sees, before she runs off to help Mami and Tía Lola carry in the rest of the platters from the kitchen. It's only later, thinking back over Miguel's puzzling grin, that Juanita realizes that her brother's remark wasn't exactly a compliment.

● ● ●

"Please, everybody, serve yourselves from the buffet on the dining-room table, then go out to the rain porch and take a seat," Mami directs her guests. "Oh, and try to sit next to someone you don't know very well, okay?" It's a fine and dandy thought, but a little later Mami sits down beside Víctor. Glancing at Mami's radiant face, Juanita understands why. Víctor is a new and special friend whom Mami wants to get to know a lot better.

"Everybody has a fork and a knife and a spoon inside your napkin." Cari has stood up on a chair to make her own announcement. She demonstrates, unwrapping a sample packet. When everyone claps appreciatively, Cari's little face turns crimson with pleasure. Juanita can see how big a deal this is for Cari. With two older sisters, it must be hard to feel important or good at anything. "Hey, Cari, come sit by me," she calls out to the little girl, who has filled her plate and is now looking around for a seat in the crowded room.

Cari hurries over to the space Juanita has just made beside her at the table. It's amazing how instantly forgiving she is, as if Juanita's kind gesture has completely erased her earlier unkindness. "I love how you wrapped everything together," Juanita praises the little girl. "Where'd you get the idea?"

"I was making a silverware family," Cari explains. "First, I started with the papa knife, and then came the mama fork and then the little baby spoon." She demonstrates again with her own set and beams up at Juanita when she is done.

How did Cari get to be *so* adorable? Or was she this adorable when she was being annoying? Juanita feels another sudden gush of love just like she did for her brother. "I wish you were my little sister," she says. She really means it.

"Me too," Cari says, putting her spoon beside Juanita's to make silverware sisters.

The two girls plow into their delicious, self-served meal—a wonderful thing about parties: parents too distracted to insist on a serving of vegetables or a bigger piece of meat. Cari's plate is piled high with French fries, surrounded by a pool of ketchup, and that's it. Juanita opted for Tía Lola's luscious *pastelitos,* cheese sticks, and a hot dog destined for Valentino. The conversation turns to tadpoles and frogs, slimy stuff that Juanita would prefer not to discuss while she is eating. But Juanita is feeling so pleased with how pretty the Fourth of July bouquets turned out, how everyone has been enjoying the garden, that things that would usually annoy her just don't seem to have that effect on her at all.

Across the table from Cari and Juanita, Victoria is listening politely to a really boring baseball story some guy is telling her. Victoria has got to be the nicest person, always taking care of everybody. In fact, normally, Victoria would have reached over and wiped the ketchup off little Cari's T-shirt. She would have insisted that Cari include more of the food pyramid on her plate. Of course, Victoria hasn't touched her own food, so she can hardly complain about her little sister.

The story finally comes to an end with a flurry of home runs and a win for the home team. "That's awesome, Owen," Victoria congratulates him. Owen . . . Owen . . . the name sounds familiar. That's right: Owen is Dean's older brother, who has been helping Rudy coach the team. And suddenly, like a last puzzle piece snapping into place so she can see the whole picture, Juanita understands why Victoria has forsaken Tía Lola's summer camp to go down to the pasture to watch a bunch of boys play baseball.

●●●

"I ate too much," Essie groans from the other end of the table.

"I didn't!" Cari exclaims.

"That's because you only ate French fries!" Essie blurts out. Everyone laughs. Juanita glances at Cari, hoping she won't feel ridiculed and burst into tears. Essie can sometimes have a big mouth, just like Juanita this morning, not thinking how her words might hurt somebody's feelings. Maybe Essie is also afraid she's going to be squeezed out of any attention. But maybe now that she has been getting lots of compliments on her baseball skills, Essie will be nicer about sharing the spotlight.

"You *only* ate French fries?" Victoria has overheard Essie's comment and is suddenly all attention, her forehead creased. She has been forgetting her responsibilities as the eldest, in charge of her little sister. "Oh, Cari, you know you have to eat a balanced meal."

"But it's the Fourth of July," Cari explains.

"I guess you're right." Victoria smiles indulgently. "That shirt certainly looks like you got wounded in battle."

This is what gives Juanita the idea to include the little girl in her plans. Cari can be a wounded soldier from the War of Independence with her bloody T-shirt and her sword, even though Juanita's pretty sure that soldiers had guns back then. Juanita is glad for the company. She has been feeling increasing stage fright about getting the whole room's attention just to herself. Meanwhile, Cari is thrilled to be part of Juanita's surprise and suggests wearing a bloody ketchup bandage around her head and limping like Miguel does when he tries walking on his hurt foot.

Maybe it's because the fireworks were canceled or because these guests had nowhere else to go this Fourth of July, or else they wouldn't have been free to accept this last-minute invitation, but Juanita's and Cari's surprise is especially appreciated.

With a flare of trumpets (from a CD Mami has) and a clang of cymbals (from the pot and metal spoon Tía Lola is holding), a wounded Revolutionary War soldier comes down the stairs. She is wielding a sword to defend the home of the brave, or so she announces to the huddled masses yearning to breathe free. Behind the soldier is a noble beast with a red bandanna, carrying a little American flag in his mouth. Then, straight from the harbor of New York City, Lady Liberty makes her entrance in her star hat and her white robe and a tablet on which are written the words of "The Star-Spangled Banner," because they're kind of hard to remember. In fact, for the longest time, Juanita thought the song was addressed to Miguel's friend José, in New York City: "José, can you see . . ." But then Ms. Sweeney told her class the story, explaining what ramparts were and what a perilous fight was. Everyone had to write out the first verse, an assignment on which Juanita got an A for her beautiful penmanship.

Lady Liberty sings the national anthem, with the wounded soldier coming in for the parts she knows. One by one, folks start joining in. Colonel Charlebois, dressed as usual in his old army uniform, struggles to his feet and puts his hand on his heart. When they get to the bombs bursting in air, Valentino lets out a series of explosive barks that makes the room roar with laughter.

Tía Lola enters from the kitchen with a cake decorated with candles and tiny American flags. Everyone now joins in singing "Happy Birthday" to the United States, including Tía Lola, who feels especially grateful to this great country for letting her stay with her family and all the new friends she has made.

"Make a wish!" Tía Lola reminds everybody, before Colonel Charlebois does the honors and blows out the candles.

Juanita closes her eyes. Earlier today, there were a zillion wishes she would have made. But right now she can't think of anything else that would make this a more special day! The only thing missing is Papi, but he called up just a little while ago to say that he and Carmen and Abuelito and Abuelita are coming this weekend to see them and also watch Miguel's baseball game.

It's dark by the time the last guest leaves. As Juanita and her family stand in the front yard waving goodbye, one little light, then another, and another, then more and more, twinkle in the darkness. "They're fireflies!" Juanita explains because none of the Swords have actually ever seen them.

Well, Essie claims she saw some the night they were out on the treasure hunt. But she thought she was seeing stars like when you spin yourself around too many times and almost pass out.

"Why are they lighting up like that?" Cari wants to know.

"Mother Nature is giving us her especial fireworks," Tía Lola tells the little girl.

Juanita can't help smiling. She got her fireworks after all! Back inside, she collects her costume and cleans off her sword, still muddy from the garden, to take up to her room. When Tía Lola notices the blank blade, she offers Juanita her marker, as she did with Cari.

"What for?" Juanita doesn't need her name on a sword to feel special anymore.

Six

wednesday

Victorious Vicky

Victoria lies in bed, enjoying a rare treat. In the next bed, Cari is still fast asleep. As soon as she wakes, it'll be Victoria's responsibility to help her little sister dress, accompany her downstairs, and get her to eat some breakfast, including going through the daily struggle about the need for milk for calcium for her growing bones. What a relief just to lie in bed daydreaming, not worrying about anyone or anything!

But then a little worry cloud sails into Victoria's head. How on earth is she going to get out of Tía Lola's summer camp outing today? They're all supposed to drive over to Fort Ticonderoga, a military museum, where there's going to be a Revolutionary War reenactment. It was her father's idea, the big history fan. Papa is so excited and thinks this is such a special treat. Honestly! Why would anyone want to go watch grown men dressed in costumes shoot at each other with noisy muskets? She'll be bored to tears.

It's true that Victoria used to feel the same way about baseball. But now that Owen has explained to her all the intricacies of the game, she is a total fan. As she tried to tell him yesterday, if it hadn't been for him . . . She was about to finish her sentence when she made the mistake of looking into his blue eyes. They had this soft, mesmerizing home-run glow to them.

Victoria doesn't want to hurt her father's feelings, but she really would prefer if Papa and Cari and Mami and Tía Lola and Juanita went by themselves. Hopefully, Miguel's ankle will be cured, so that Essie will want to go, too. Victoria is pretty sure her sister won't turn down the chance to watch an actual battle, given that she's always starting them. Besides, it'll be so annoying if Essie stays. Her sister is constantly pestering Owen with baseball questions, hogging all the attention. And Victoria has so much to talk to Owen about before she has to leave Vermont on Sunday.

She could try acting sick, but that might totally backfire on her. Her worrywart father would not only cancel the outing, but stick around insisting Victoria stay in bed. Any chance of seeing Owen today would evaporate. The best policy, as her father is always telling her, is honesty.

But Victoria has such a hard time telling people stuff they don't want to hear and seeing them be upset with her or unhappy with themselves. She can't bear it! If only she could get rid of that part of herself! Be free to be her fun, exciting, perky, selfish self! She punches her pillow a bunch of times, then buries her face in it, stifling her screams (otherwise she'll wake up Cari): I hate being the responsible, thoughtful, helpful, polite one! Oh, Owen, Owen, Owen, please save me, oh save me from this cruel destiny of being the oldest!

● ● ●

One flight down, Tía Lola is cooking breakfast. Today it's a Dominican treat, *mangú*, a dish made of mashed plantains, with a special fried cheese Rudy is kind enough to order from his Boston supplier. A hearty breakfast for people going to watch a bloody battle or play baseball.

But as she is finishing up the dish, Tía Lola distinctly feels a little sword jabbing at her heart. One of her campers is experiencing trouble. Who can it be? Probably Miguel. He has been growing impatient with how slowly his ankle is healing. Tía Lola turns off the stove, dries her hands on her apron, and heads upstairs.

As she reaches the second floor, the guest room door opens. The oldest of Víctor's girls, the lovely Victoria, is tiptoeing out. She gives a little jump when she sees she is not alone.

"Sorry," Tía Lola mouths. She would continue her trek upstairs to check on Miguel, but something desperate in the girl's face makes her stop. She gestures for Victoria to come up to her attic room. For a moment, Victoria looks unsure, but then with a sigh of relief, she nods.

71

● ● ●

Working as a team, Victoria and Tía Lola manage to talk Mami and Víctor and the three girls into going to Fort Ticonderoga without them.

At first, Essie keeps changing her mind. Miguel's ankle is still swollen. She would love to substitute for a second day, but she'd also love to watch a real-life battle. "I've heard it's like a show in Disney World," her older sister remarks. That clinches it.

As for Tía Lola staying behind: "I'd love a quiet day working in my garden." It's so rare that Tía Lola asks for something, no one thinks to talk her out of it.

"How did you do that?" Victoria whispers. Tía Lola shrugs like she doesn't know what big thing she just did. "Tell everyone what you wanted without apologizing?" Victoria elaborates.

"I just told everyone what I wanted without apologizing," Tía Lola laughs. Like it's that simple. "Now you try it."

But Victoria isn't so sure she can withstand her father's persistence. "Are you certain you want to stay, Victoria?" he keeps asking. Each time, she can feel her certainty eroding. "It'll be a chance to see our country's history in action."

Papa, pleeeeeeease!!! Victoria feels like shouting. I have ZERO interest in watching any history except my own in action!!!

Tía Lola steps in. "Victoria'll keep me company and help me take care of our patient."

Of course Papa has to bring up some hurdles. "But

neither of you can carry Miguel. And Rudy can't do it either. Remember, he's not a young man. Come to think of it . . ." Oh no! Papa himself is reconsidering. Unless Tía Lola and Victoria think of something quick, the whole outing will be canceled.

"Owen can carry him," Victoria blurts out, an edge of desperation in her voice.

Mami has also been pushing for Victoria to come along. But just this moment, Mami must see something she didn't see before. Victoria is blushing at the mere mention of Dean's tall, handsome fourteen-year-old brother.

"Víctor, I actually will feel a lot better leaving Miguel in Victoria's hands," Mami says, looping her arm through his and escorting him out to the van.

As they drive off, Victoria could swear that Linda calls out, "Have a lovely time with Ow—I mean, Miguel."

●●●

Throughout this parting scene, Miguel looks on grimly. He dislikes being cast in the role of wounded athlete needing care. He doesn't need care. He needs his ankle back in shape so he can play baseball this Saturday.

What's making Miguel feel even more desperate is that Papi called yesterday to announce that he and Carmen, Abuelito, and Abuelita are all coming this weekend to watch his first big game. Miguel was still counting on his miracle, so he didn't mention his injury. Amazingly, neither did Juanita, who has to be the world's biggest blabbermouth. But then, his little sister was acting super-weird, going around hugging people and telling them how much she loved them.

As for Mami, she was too busy to talk long with Papi. She did say she'd make them all a reservation at the B&B down the road. Papi must have asked if there was any way they could all stay together at the house like last time. Of course that would have been fine, but Mami explained how right now all the bedrooms were occupied, as Víctor was up visiting with his girls. This really surprised Papi, as Mami later recounted, which Miguel doesn't understand, since Carmen and Víctor work in the same law practice. Plus, they're friends. Surely, he must have mentioned coming to Vermont. But maybe not. The more Miguel knows of grown-ups, the weirder they seem. Only his little sister is weirder, but at least she doesn't get to boss him around.

But none of these plans will matter if his ankle hasn't healed. Papi will probably cancel his trip altogether. Maybe on account of hanging out so much with Víctor, Miguel wants to feel that Papi will always be his father, no matter what happens between Víctor and Mami.

"What am I going to do, Tía Lola?" he asks his aunt once the Fort Ticonderoga contingent has left.

"Remember how with patience and calm, even a donkey can climb a palm tree!" A favorite saying of hers. "It's just going to take a little more time for your ankle to heal, just as it's going to take a little more time for you to grow taller. These things will come, I promise."

But Miguel's patience is wearing thin. Good thing Tía

Lola invites Dean and his brother, Owen, to come over for lunch before practice, because that takes Miguel's mind off the thought that some donkeys who try to climb up palm trees probably don't succeed.

●●●

It *is* a lovely day for Victoria.

The only part she feels bad about is that she didn't just tell her father the truth. Papa, she should have said, I want some time to myself; I want to get to know this nice boy; I want to do fun things on my own without always having to include my younger sisters. It's such a relief to talk to Tía Lola. She listens and doesn't make Victoria feel like a selfish brat. It's a little like having her mother back. But even saying that much might make Papa sad.

"Next time you will tell him more of the truth," Tía Lola reassures Victoria as they prepare lunch together. "You're taking little baby steps, and like Miguel with his ankle, you have to be patient." Tía Lola is like a life coach! "*Hay que darle tiempo al tiempo.* You know that expression?"

Victoria winces as if she were Miguel stepping on his bad foot. "My mother used to say that," she explains in a pained voice. " 'You have to give time to time.' " And just like that, Victoria is sobbing in Tía Lola's arms. It's a good thing that Owen and Dean and Miguel are out in the living room, watching some game on ESPN. "I'm sorry," Victoria keeps saying, but Tía Lola tells her there is nothing at all to be sorry about. She understands how hard it is for Victoria to be growing up without her mother.

Before joining the boys, Victoria washes her face. "Do I look like I've been crying?"

"Yes, you do. And it makes your brown eyes shinier and your face prettier." Tía Lola has a way of telling the truth that doesn't hurt to hear it.

"*Ay,* Tía Lola!" Victoria throws her arms around her wonderful new friend. "I hope we do move to Vermont!"

Tía Lola hugs the sweet girl back. "I hope so, too!" That would be the best miracle of all: if Linda and Víctor were to fall in love.

●●●

"What's with the swords?" Owen wants to know as they head to the back field. Miguel and Victoria have insisted on bringing along these Halloween swords. Owen is serving as Miguel's crutch on the right, while Victoria is on the left. Tía Lola follows, carrying a small stool on which Miguel will rest his bad foot.

"The swords are *una tradición latina,*" Tía Lola says playfully. A Latin tradition? "*Ay, sí, Owensito,*" she teases, calling him "little Owen," when he towers above her. "You know how the valentine angel carries love arrows?" She must mean Cupid. "*Bueno,* before a game or a practice, we Latinos carry harmless swords to remind us to play fair and make friends."

"Awesome," he says, but suddenly the only three Latinos he has ever known are laughing. "What?" he asks, baffled.

"I am pulling your toes," Tía Lola explains. She often gets her English expressions mixed up.

"You mean pulling his leg, Tía Lola," Victoria offers when she manages to stop laughing.

"It was only a little joke I play on Owensito," Tía Lola explains, "so I only pulled his toes this time, but next time, he better watch out that I don't cut off his head."

She brandishes her sword like she means business. Owen ducks, pretending to defend himself. In doing so, he lets go of Miguel's right side, so that accidentally, Miguel steps on his sore foot. And what a surprise: the ankle is tender, but it doesn't really hurt him anymore!

By the time the British regiment has shot its first cannon, and the light infantry has marched across the green at Fort Ticonderoga, the team has been practicing for an hour and is ready for a break. Tía Lola and Victoria come down from the house with a tray of homemade cookies and two pitchers of lemonade.

"Where is the *coronel*?" Tía Lola asks, looking around. Colonel Charlebois usually shows up at the team's practices.

"Down with a cold," Rudy sighs. It was a job convincing the old man to take a day off. "How's our other wounded soldier?" Rudy asks, nodding at Miguel's foot.

"Super!" Miguel demonstrates, taking a few tentative steps. He is so ready to play ball.

But Rudy isn't sure that ankle is ready. "I hate to be the

heavy here, Captain. But how about we give it one more day?"

Miguel shoots Owen a desperate look. But as the assistant, Owen has to back up his coach. Owen relates how he himself messed up his pitching arm last year by playing too soon after an injury. You'd think he almost died or something; Victoria looks like she's about to faint.

"Owen's right, Miguel," Victoria pleads. "Please, just one more day, please." She looks almost as worried about Miguel as she did about Owen.

The truth is that it's hard to resist a pretty girl acting like you'll break her heart if you ignore her request. It helps that she sits down beside him on the bench, needing a lot of help with the rules and moves of baseball.

One thing leads to another, and before long, Miguel is telling Victoria about his apprehensions for the weekend.

"What exactly are you worried about?" She is such a good listener, letting him finish without interrupting, thinking about what he says before responding.

"I was worried that I wouldn't get to play at all. Now I guess I'm afraid we'll lose. I also worry Papi might feel bad about your father and my mother." He doesn't want to sound like he is criticizing Víctor, whom he actually likes a lot, which is part of the problem. Feeling like he's not being loyal to Papi.

"But didn't you say your father and Carmen are engaged to be married?"

"I know." Miguel shrugs. He picks up his sword lying beside him and whips it a few times in the air. "You know what I'd do if this sword *were* magic? I'd use it to get rid of worries. Wham, wham, wham!"

Victoria is smiling at him. "So, what's holding you back, *Michael*?" she teases. Just then she hears an echo deep inside her, asking, So, what's holding *you* back, Vicky?

●●●

That night at dinner, everyone is full of stories of their lovely day. The Fort Ticonderoga contingent almost go to battle themselves over which was the most exciting part of the reenactment: the redcoats firing their cannons, or the infantrymen marching in formation, or the colonials ambushing them just beyond the refreshments stand, or the loyalists waving their white flags in surrender.

The stay-at-home group listen tolerantly. They don't seem in the least bit envious, which is odd. After all, they didn't get to watch the birth of the United States of America right before their very eyes and on the day after the Fourth of July. Miguel didn't even get to play baseball, spending a second day just watching from the sidelines. Meanwhile, all Victoria got to do was help Tía Lola bake cookies and make lunch and lemonade. But no matter how much more gore Essie piles on, or how much Cari stresses how very scary it was, or how much history Papa emphasizes she missed out on, Victoria seems unimpressed. In fact, she looks like she might be stifling a yawn.

"Well, next time, Victoria, you'll have to come," Papa states, as if it's a sure thing.

"We'll see," Victoria answers back, just like a grown-up.

Her father blinks, surprised by the response. "I mean it, Victoria. You would definitely enjoy it."

"How would you know, Papa?" Victoria's voice has suddenly acquired an edge. "Don't you think I should know more than you what I would really enjoy?" She pushes her chair back from the table with an earsplitting screech. The room has gone absolutely still. Everyone is shocked at the transformation in the sweet eldest Sword. As if astonished herself, Victoria bursts into tears and runs out of the room. They hear her footsteps trotting across the living room and out into the mudroom. *Bang* goes the front door with that extra force that says: I am slamming this in case you missed how upset I am!

Víctor is on his feet. He intends to go after his daughter and remind her that she is the eldest, and they are guests, and she owes everyone an apology. But Tía Lola intervenes. "I think right now the best thing for Victoria is to have a little time to herself."

Víctor runs his hand through his hair. Suddenly, there seems to be more gray peppering the black. He looks confounded. Unlike Essie, his eldest is the soul of gentleness, so willing to please. "Did something happen today to upset her?"

"No, actually, Victoria had a lovely day," Tía Lola says, winking at Mami.

"Do sit down, Víctor, and let's talk," Mami says, reaching for his hand. Víctor seems soothed by her touch and sits back down. "Girls and boys," Mami says, although the only boy here is Miguel, "could you go out in the backyard and get the campfire ready for s'mores, okay?"

"Let me carry you out, Miguel," Víctor says, starting to get up again.

"I'm good," Miguel assures him. How it happened, Miguel can't say, but his ankle really does feel okay. Later, he'll soak it in a solution with salts that Tía Lola has prepared for him. It looks like his donkey will make it to the top of that palm tree today.

●●●

A little while later, Victoria reenters the house on tiptoe. After she washes her face so she doesn't look like she has been crying, she goes in search of everybody. The rooms are deserted. Where did everyone go? They probably all got in the car and drove off to . . . to . . . Fort Ticonderoga to have a great time without her. Good riddance! She'd like a little time to herself, if they want to know the truth.

But the truth is that when you finally get a little time to yourself, it is nice to know that at the other end of it, you will find the people you love waiting for you, glad to have you back, eager to hear your stories. So instead of marching upstairs, wrapped in a righteous mantle, Victoria calls out, "Papa? Cari? Essie? Tía Lola?"

Room to room she goes with growing apprehension. Where are they? And then she hears their bright voices coming up from the backyard. What a warm surge of happiness to look out the window and see them gathered together, safe and sound. They've even got a real campfire going!

But perhaps because she is her father's daughter, the happiness is tinged with worry. What if they won't take her back? Or what if they take her back, and she is again imprisoned inside that sweet, polite, responsible Victoria?

With luck, she'll be fine. But just in case, she decides to retrieve her sword from the big flowerpot full of umbrellas in the mudroom where she plunged it when she came back from running away. Every time she sees that playful, perky name, Vicky, on the blade, she thinks, That's not me. But come to think of it, the name does fit. Victoria has been searching for the Vicky part of herself for years. Today she has found her.

"Let's go!" she says out loud, flourishing her sword as if she were leading a charge against the oppressive British. She needs to work up her courage before facing the people who have loved her as Victoria and will also love her as Vicky.

Seven

thursday

Esperanza's Dashing Hopes

Esperanza Espada, a.k.a. Hope Sword, may not be in Disney World, but she sure has been having an insane rollercoaster ride all the same.

First, she was *down* about coming to Vermont. But upon arrival, Tía Lola announced her summer camp idea, which was an *uplifting* surprise. The nighttime treasure hunt turned out to be quite fun. Then Miguel got hurt, which Essie knows was a downswing of his personal roller coaster, but hers just about peaked. She was able to play baseball and be as good as, if not better than, some of the team. But actually, yesterday's trip to Fort Ticonderoga was tops. Who would have thought that in the middle of nowhere there'd be a place as cool as Disney World?

But the problem with being at the top is that a bottom will inevitably come. And that's what this Thursday morning is turning out to be. Miguel wakes up with a healed ankle, raring to go. Even before breakfast, he's out there with Papa, hitting balls, catching, throwing. He's my father, Essie feels like reminding them both.

Then, at breakfast, Papa asks Victoria what she'd like to do today. "Just watch baseball practice, I guess," she says in a small voice, as if she's afraid to speak up, though she had no problem at all yesterday. Meanwhile, Papa has been enlisted to help coach, mostly running extra drills for Miguel so he can catch up. That leaves only Essie, Juanita, and Cari to participate in Tía Lola's camp today, which means the activity has to be something that little kids can keep up with. How much fun can that be for Essie? It'll be like babysitting without even getting paid for it!

No two ways about it: Essie's hopes for today are dashed. She feels like taking that supposedly magic sword and just snapping it in two to show what she thinks of miracles. What no one knows, not even Juanita because she had already fallen asleep, is that last night, Essie secretly slipped her sword under her pillow and wished for three things: First, that Miguel wouldn't be able to play today, so that Essie could fill in. Second, that Miguel wouldn't be able to play Friday either. And third, you get her drift? That Miguel wouldn't be able to play on Saturday, and Essie would step in and help the team win their big game.

Essie knows that she wouldn't be able to substitute if this were an official Little League team. But Charlie's Boys is just a collection of local kids wanting to play baseball after their Little League season is over. What's more, with teammates on summer trips, the team doesn't even always have substitute players. The one dependable substitute, Patrick, is the worst player. In fact, Essie has been taking him aside and teaching him stuff. All Essie is asking her sword for is to let her be a second or third substitute. It's not a biggie miracle, for heaven's sake. She's not asking to go to Disney World, or to get her mother back, or to make Cari stop stealing all the attention. One crummy chance to be a star baseball player in front of her new friends in Vermont.

Incredible as it seems, Essie has made friends in this place she was determined to dislike. Juanita, for one. Much as Essie complains, there are some pluses to having a younger friend: Juanita almost always lets Essie take the lead. Essie also likes the guys in Charlie's Boys. They've been complimentary, never adding "for a girl" when they say Essie's a great hitter or an amazing pitcher. She considers Miguel her friend as well, even if he is standing in the way of her hopes. She admires how he puts his team first, something she would find hard to do. He's real smart, too, guessing all those clues for the treasure hunt. Most of all, Essie loves Tía Lola because she is like a Mary Poppins aunt who can take the most boring activity in the world and somehow turn it into fun.

That's why Essie doesn't sink into total despair this Thursday morning, even though it looks like her wishes are not going to come true. Sure enough, Tía Lola announces that for today's camp outing, they are going to bike into town to the municipal pool, swim for a couple of hours, then head over to Amigos Café for lunch. In the afternoon, they'll visit some of Tía Lola's friends in town.

"Like who?" Essie wants to know.

"Oh, let's see. Estargazer."

Cool, Stargazer owns a totally fun gift shop.

"Then we'll visit *el coronel* Charlebois, who is sick, *pobrecito.*" The poor old man already missed baseball practice yesterday. "*El coronel* just caught a little cold from all this wet weather. He gets lonesome by himself when he can't get out." Tía Lola can understand. Before she started teaching Spanish at Miguel and Juanita's school, she used to get so sad cooped up in the house by herself all day long. "We are to have tea and cookies at his home."

"Is that the house that looks haunted?" Cari's eyes widen. Every time they go to town, Cari begs to drive by it so she can get a Halloween thrill right in the middle of summer.

"*Ay,* Cari, *querida,* do not worry. That house is haunted only by memories," Tía Lola assures her. "*El coronel* Charlebois has traveled all over the world and has wonderful stories to tell."

That could be kind of fun, Essie is thinking. Colonel Charlebois has led an exciting life, from what Essie has heard, fighting real battles, being a hero. He has also amassed a considerable amount of money. From the few books Essie has read on her own—okay, she's not as big a reader as Juanita—she knows rich, elderly bachelors usually leave their money to somebody. Essie also knows the old man really loves baseball, and he seemed very impressed with her playing during practice on the Fourth of July. So maybe Colonel Charlebois will leave her a million dollars so that she can buy her own baseball team and a big, huge piece of land   probably in Vermont—where she can build her very own diamond.

From dashed hopes, Essie's state of mind has taken a decidedly upward swing. As she rolls her sword in her beach towel and stuffs it into her backpack, she is thinking maybe it didn't let her down after all. Maybe it has an even better fate in store for her. "Cancel last night's wishes," she whispers, and then she tells her sword what she is really, really hoping for.

They ride in, Juanita on her bike, and Cari in a red wagon Tía Lola rigged behind her bike, and Essie on Miguel's. With her swimsuit under her clothes and her sword sticking out of her backpack, Essie feels the thrill of adventure. Maybe she'll just keep going, a bicycle hobo, cycling all the way down to Disney World in Florida. Only thing is, how will the lawyers reach her to inform her that she just inherited a million dollars from Colonel Charlebois? Essie wishes Papa weren't so strict and had gotten her a cell phone.

For right now, Essie is happy just being at the municipal pool. Swimming is always fun, but what makes it more special today is that Essie is also making friends. Maybe it's because she's from New York City, but Essie is like an instant celebrity. Just in the space of an hour, she has added four new friends to her life, and Essie would have to struggle to name four kids in her fifth-grade class in Queens that she could call a friend. Essie doesn't mean to be unpleasant, but she has a tendency to argue a lot, and nobody seems to like that. But here in Vermont, she hasn't found that much to argue about.

Being with Tía Lola also helps. People just flock to her, even though she doesn't know much English. Many kids even try to talk to her in Spanish, which surprises Essie, but it turns out Tía Lola was their Spanish teacher this past year.

Essie also meets the Prouty twins, who have *horses,* and they invite Essie to come over whenever she wants to ride them. There's a boy, Milton, from Juanita's class, who asks Essie a lot of questions about the city, but then when Essie finds out he lives on a farm, she fires back a bunch of her own, and between answering and asking, they can't stop talking to each other.

A quiet girl listens in like their audience. Her name is Hannah, which is kind of funny that she should have the same name as Hannah Montana, a movie star, when she's so shy. But then, parents have to name their kids before they have any idea what that little baby will be like. Look at her with a name like Esperanza, which even in English, Hope, is a name for a goody-goody-two-shoes. That's not Essie at all! If her mother and father had known what she was going to be like, they would probably have named her Contrary. That's what Papa is always accusing her of being, contrary, as in not always the easiest person to get along with.

After swimming, the camp group heads over to the café.

Rudy hasn't left yet for practice, so he has lunch right along with them. Without Victoria around, Essie is free to ask as many baseball questions as she can think of without being reminded that she needs to give Rudy a break so he can eat his lunch. Cari and Juanita are more than glad to have Essie talk while they eat up all the French fries. "Hey! No fair!" she says, slapping their hands away playfully. When Essie is a millionaire, she's going to hire a chef who specializes in French fries, pizza, macaroni and cheese, and desserts with chocolate. She'll kiss the food pyramid goodbye forever.

They stroll through town after lunch. "Good for the digestion," Tía Lola claims. Even better for the digestion is stopping at Stargazer's store! They can touch anything in the shop, turn it on, play with it. Stargazer doesn't seem to mind. She's too busy talking to Tía Lola about their auras, whole body-size halos that Stargazer can read. Essie wonders if Stargazer might look at her and see money in her future.

As they walk over to Colonel Charlebois' house, Essie's head is spinning. She'll have to pay close attention to the rooms so she can start planning how she is going to redecorate them once she moves up to Vermont to be a millionaire. Wait a minute! Did she just actually wish to *stay* in Vermont? Is this the same girl who a week ago was sure it was a death sentence to visit, much less stay in, Vermont? Sometimes Essie has to agree with what she knows is the general opinion in her family: it's not always easy being with Essie. But if they think that's hard, they should try *being* Essie and having to be with herself all the time!

●●●

Colonel Charlebois is expecting them. He has a tea tray all laid out in a room he calls the parlor.

"Sit down and make yourselves comfortable." Colonel Charlebois gestures toward an assembly of stiff-backed chairs.

The invitation is easier said than followed, as the furniture proves to be very uncomfortable, like you are sitting at attention. The air smells musty. The house is not haunted—Cari doesn't have to be looking around with big spooked eyes—but it is dark and sad and somber, a house that never gets to hear kids laughing or arguing, dogs barking, never gets to smell potatoes being fried up or a cake baking in the oven.

The mood seizes Essie in a way she didn't expect. Now she wants Colonel Charlebois to adopt her so she can come up here and throw open the windows and paint the walls bright colors and replace the furniture with beanbags and puffy couches you can fall into while watching a big-screen TV. That would be the first thing Essie'd buy, as the small one in the corner probably doesn't even have a remote control. But mostly, Essie would sit down with the sad-looking old man, as she does now, and ask him a whole bunch of questions about when he traveled around the world and what he had to do to become a hero.

"That was a long time ago." Colonel Charlebois waves her questions away at first. His hands are so shaky that the little teacups rattle violently when he picks them up to

90

pour tea in them. Tía Lola very tactfully intervenes. "Just so you can talk, *coronel*."

"It'll bore you all to tears, then you'll never come back to visit me. Now go ahead and eat some cookies." The old man has such a bossy way of talking. Nobody would think of contradicting him.

Except Essie. "If we thought we'd be bored to tears, we wouldn't be asking, now would we?"

The colonel's jaw drops. Essie can hear the little click of his old dentures. Then he is laughing so hard, it brings on a fit of horrible-sounding coughing.

"I can see you hit them back not only in baseball," he says once he has recovered. There's a sparkle in his eye and a smile on his thin lips. Even with his bad cough and his heavy sweater-vest in the middle of summer, Essie can see that the old man is already feeling better with the company.

Soon the colonel is launched on a journey down memory lane, taking three rapt girls and a delighted Tía Lola along. The room is transformed into a Korean jungle, a Japanese temple, a Saharan desert, shark-infested waters off the coast of India, the high seas where pirate ships prowl in search of friendly vessels, and submarines slice the darkness fathoms beyond where sunlight ever reaches. Now it's Essie's jaw dropping with wonder.

Upon Cari's request, Colonel Charlebois gives them a tour of the house. They end up in an attic storeroom with a closet full of old mothball-smelling uniforms hanging in a row and boxes stuffed with what the colonel calls memorabilia and a bunch of medals. There's also a dragon mask from China, a snake charmer's basket from India, and a ceremonial sword in a fanciful scabbard with a tassel, given to him by a Japanese official whose family used to be samurai warriors.

"Awesome!" Essie says. "It's like another Excalibur!"

"What's an excantaloupe?" Cari asks.

Essie sighs with impatience. "Excalibur is like *the* most famous sword in history. It belonged to King Arthur."

Cari doesn't know who King Arthur is either, but she's not going to ask Essie another question and be made to feel even dumber.

"So, can I hold it?" Essie asks in a breathless voice.

"Of course," Colonel Charlebois says, unsheathing the beautiful weapon. As Essie strikes a pose, Colonel Charlebois laughs. "By the way, am I mistaken, or did I see that you yourself had a sword sticking out of your backpack?"

Essie is so mesmerized by the sword, for once she doesn't speak right up.

"We all have them." Juanita has been trying to get a word in edgewise since the visit started. "Tía Lola gave them to us."

"They're supposed to be magic and help us with a . . . a . . ." Cari can't remember the word Papa used. Something about girdles.

"Help with a challenge," Tía Lola explains. "Like when you, Cari, needed extra courage, or you, Juanita, needed to feel like you were especial."

"Those are certainly valuable swords if they can accomplish so much." Colonel Charlebois sounds impressed. "This one is only good for murder and plunder."

Essie finally cedes the sword so Cari and Juanita can also hold it and strike poses and imagine themselves as samurai warriors. The afternoon begins to turn to evening. By the time they are ready to leave, it really is too late to ride their bikes home.

Colonel Charlebois comes up with a plan. "How about I give you all a ride now, and then tomorrow, I'll pick you up, and you can ride your bikes back home? I get a second visit out of it."

"But your cold, *coronel*," Tía Lola reminds him. He really should not go out with a cold in the damp evening air.

"Nonsense! I've never felt better in my life," the colonel says gruffly. "What's more, I've had one of the most entertaining afternoons of my life, and I wouldn't mind repeating it. Now, the sooner we get in the car, the faster we'll get there." It's like he's still in the army, barking out orders. Watching him, Essie wonders whom he reminds her of. And then she realizes: me!

Soon another treat awaits her: Essie has been hoping to ride in Colonel Charlebois' wonderful silver car as big as a tank. The hood ornament is a little silver batter from when the colonel was part of an army baseball team in Panama, called Los Dorados. They won so many trophies, each player got to take one home. The colonel put his on his new Cadillac Eldorado, which he bought precisely because it had a similar name as his team. They heard all about his posting in Panama this afternoon. That's where he picked up his Spanish.

Like a gentleman, Colonel Charlebois insists on holding the door open for everyone. But before getting in, he remembers something he has to get in the house. Whatever it is, it goes in the trunk, and then he's back, turning on the car. The engine sounds a little like it is having its very own coughing fit. Away they go, Colonel Charlebois telling about some championship game in Panama when the bases were loaded and he was up to bat. "Ever been south of the border?" he asks Essie.

"I was thinking of riding my bike all the way to Florida," Essie confides.

Colonel Charlebois is intrigued. So Essie elaborates about being a hobo and not having to attend school and getting to go to Disney World, since plane tickets for her whole family are too expensive. The colonel listens carefully, like he is just as enchanted by Essie's stories as she is by his.

"What made you change your mind?"

How does Essie tell him about the million dollars she was hoping to inherit from him? How if she was on the road without a cell phone, the lawyers couldn't reach her to give her the news? The last thing in the world Essie would want to do is hurt the colonel's feelings by mentioning something as rude as his death. He'd think she was eager to visit and listen to his stories only because she wanted his money. For the second time in an afternoon, Essie doesn't have a whole lot to say.

"I guess I changed my mind on account of I'd miss my

family too much." Once she says so, Essie knows it's the truth.

"Wise choice," the colonel says thoughtfully. "One that sometimes I wish I had made. But that's neither here nor there. We make our beds and we have to lie in them."

"It's never too late to buy a softer mattress or change for a bigger model!" Tía Lola reminds him, laughing.

They pull up to the house, already wrapped in that soft haze of a summer evening. Colonel Charlebois agrees to stay for dinner. By the time he is ready to leave, it's already dark. He asks Essie if she wouldn't mind accompanying him to the car. He has something for her in the trunk.

Essie's heart soars. She is going to get a gift from Colonel Charlebois, without him having to die first!

When Essie shines the beam of her treasure-hunt flashlight into the trunk, which the colonel has thrown open, she can hardly believe her eyes. The samurai sword in its elaborate scabbard! "For me?" she gasps. But a second later, her heart plummets. Papa will never let her accept such a precious gift. He'll think that, Essie being Essie, she must have hinted that she sure could use a samurai sword down in the dangerous streets of New York City.

"I can't," she has to admit sadly. "Papa'll make me give it back. He thinks we're imposing if people give us stuff."

"We won't call it a gift, then," Colonel Charlebois suggests.

Essie can feel the skies of possibility opening. Like when a roller coaster climbs slowly, with effort, and you know once you get to the top, you're going to plunge down, but that means you'll soon be swinging back up in a wild, wonderful arc of a ride. You need the down part to make the up part so thrilling.

"Let's just call it a trade."

A trade? But Essie doesn't have anything as special to exchange for a genuine samurai sword.

"Didn't you say you had a magic sword?"

"But it's not really, it's just a plastic—"

The colonel shakes his head. "If Tía Lola says that sword is magic, then that's guarantee enough for me. Lord knows I have a bunch of challenges I need help with right now, including this cold. So, what do you say, is it a swap or not?"

Is this really happening? Essie wonders as she races back to the house to retrieve the sword from her backpack. Before handing it over, she says, "Thank you, sword, for granting my wish." She did not inherit a million dollars or get to play baseball instead of Miguel, but she is now the proud owner of a genuine samurai warrior sword. She has also had a magnificent day and made several new friends. True to her name, Esperanza has everything she could hope for.

thursday night and friday

Mami's Mistake Monster

It's been another packed evening: dinner with Colonel Charlebois, a campfire with songs and s'mores. The kids and Tía Lola have all gone up to bed.

Mami and Víctor linger, sitting on the deck, the lights from the second-floor bedrooms shining down on them. It's their last opportunity to talk privately before more guests arrive tomorrow.

Papi and Carmen and Abuelito and Abuelita will all be staying in the house—Mami caved in to keep everyone happy. Papi will sleep on the pullout couch in the den, and the girls all together in Juanita's room, freeing up the guest room for Abuelito and Abuelita. Carmen is delighted to share a room with Tía Lola. It will be a hectic couple of

97

days, what with the big game, meals, visiting, before the guests all leave on Sunday.

Maybe that's why Victoria has been drawn to her window, already feeling so wistful about their departure. She has wished on a star and kissed the blade of her sword several times for good luck. What else can she do? She really hopes Papa will decide to relocate to Vermont. But each time the Swords have brought it up, Papa has replied, "It's not just up to me, you know."

On the deck, below Victoria's window, an interesting conversation is unfolding. Victoria wouldn't dream of snooping, but then she hears the magic words "move to Vermont." She hushes Cari and Juanita and Essie, who are jabbering away in the room behind her. They hurry to the window, curious to see what has caught the eldest Sword's attention.

"I just think we need to put the move to Vermont on hold," Linda is saying. She and Víctor met only three months ago. Since then it's been a whirlwind of phone calls, a previous visit by Víctor, and now this visit with his girls. "I just worry that everything is moving too fast for the kids. A divorce. Then their father getting engaged. And your girls, too. It's a big change from New York City to Vermont. They've been through so much in the last few years." Mami sighs as if she herself is out of breath with how many things have been happening. "I think we all need to slow down a little."

"But I don't want to slow down." Papa's voice sounds so sad, as if Linda has just given him a death sentence. "I don't get it. I think the kids are doing great. Are you sure it's not you who are having doubts?"

"Not at all!" Linda says so vehemently that Victoria can't help feeling relieved.

Her father must be relieved, too. He reaches for Linda's hand. "What's this?" he asks, lifting her hand to the light. Linda is clutching the sword Tía Lola gave her as if for dear life.

"I needed some help talking to you," Linda admits, trying to laugh it off.

"Please don't worry," Papa says. "I wouldn't move up here if I didn't think it was the best thing for everybody concerned. And I promise not to put any pressure on you. I'll wait for as long as it takes you. Only one *favorcito.*" A little favor.

"What is it?" Mami sounds afraid to ask.

"I want you to use your magic sword to slay the monster."

Essie and Juanita can't help giggling. Victoria silences them with a look. But she has to admit that it is kind of funny to hear her rational lawyer papa talking about slaying monsters. It's also funny to hear him telling someone else not to worry. Papa, the big worrier! Maybe there's something in Vermont's water that has brought about this marvelous change in her father.

"So what monster is it you want me to kill?" Linda is asking.

"The monster of making mistakes. After something doesn't go well, we sometimes get scared of trying again."

Papa can be so wise sometimes. "You're probably a little afraid to fall in love again. But you have to get past that monster. And the children will all follow your lead, I'm sure. In fact, they might even help you slay the monster if you ask for their help."

Essie's shoulders are almost up to her ears as she struggles to control her giggles. She nudges the giggling Juanita, who nudges Cari. But Cari doesn't think any of this is funny. She has been getting increasingly scared by all this talk of monsters. "I don't get it," she whispers in Victoria's ear.

"I'll explain later," Victoria whispers back.

"Is it a real monster?"

Victoria shakes her head. But her sister is still looking petrified, so Victoria sends her and the two gigglers on an errand before they ruin everything. "Go upstairs and get Tía Lola and Miguel. We need to have a summit meeting, *pronto!*"

"*Ay,* Linda, I'm sorry," Papa is apologizing. "I shouldn't be hurrying you, much as I'd like to. Every heart has its very own clock. I'll tell you what, think about it in the next couple of days. If you still feel the same way on Sunday, I will respect your decision. We'll slow down, put the move to Vermont on hold for now. A year, two, as long as it takes. But"—Víctor grabs her hand with the sword in it—"I want you to give us a fighting chance."

Papa has taken the sword from her hand and is whipping it in the air.

"What are you doing?"

"Warming it up to slay that mistake monster," he jokes.

"You think this plastic sword will do the job, eh?" Mami sounds playful but also doubtful.

"If not, I know where I can borrow a genuine samurai warrior sword."

They both burst out laughing. "Shhh," Mami hushes them both. "The children are sleeping. Shhhhhhhh!"

●●●

Oh yeah? The children are now all assembled in Juanita's room for an emergency meeting. Victoria briefs Tía Lola and Miguel on the situation and adds the information about the Sunday deadline.

"That's so unfair!" Essie is beside herself. "First we don't get to go to Disney World. Now we don't get to move to Vermont." Her gloomy side is back. The glass is not half full, it's almost empty. The roller-coaster ride will never, ever go back up again.

Her older sister won't give up so easy. "Come on, Essie. We have until Sunday."

But Sunday is only two days away! "So what do you propose?" Essie says, hoping against hope that someone will come up with a solution.

"I have an idea, I have an idea!" Juanita pipes up. She explains that earlier today at Stargazer's shop, she bought something called a mood ring. She already showed it off to Cari and Essie and Tía Lola. "You put it on and the stone changes colors to show your deepest, most secret feelings. See, like right now, it's kind of red?" Juanita unfolds the little piece of paper that came with the ring. Oh no! Red

101

means she is anxious and stressed. But actually, that makes perfect sense, given that Juanita is worrying about Mami. If the stone were to turn violet, it would mean romance, passion, marriage. "So, what if we get Mami to wear it tomorrow? Then we check at dinner and see if she's really in love. What do you think?"

Miguel thinks it's the craziest thing he's ever heard of. Wouldn't Mami already know if she loved or didn't love someone?

"But maybe your *mami* isn't sure she really loves Papa as much as he loves her, you think?" Victoria ventures. She would not want her father to get hurt for anything in the world. "I'd hate for your mother to get hurt, too," she adds. Sweet Victoria. Not wanting anyone to be unhappy. Growing up is not going to change her.

"But how are you guys going to get Mami to wear the ring?" Miguel asks. They are so rah-rah with the idea, they're forgetting this minor logistical detail.

After a moment of consideration, the girls turn to Tía Lola. "Please, *por favor,* Tía Lola," they plead. "You are our last, our only hope." They clutch their hands like damsels in distress. Tía Lola keeps shaking her head and repeating, "Everything will be fine, trust me." But finally she can't resist the pleading damsels. "Okay, I'll get her to wear it." She takes the ring and slips it on. In a second, the stone gleams pure gold!

"What in the world does that mean?" Juanita checks the instructions. But gold is not listed among the colors.

"Tía Lola, you are off the charts," Victoria declares.

For some reason, this strikes everyone's funny bone. They roar with laughter.

"All that glitters is not gold, sometimes it's Tía Lola!" Essie jokes, recalling the rhyme from the treasure hunt their first night in Vermont.

More loud laughter.

"What's going on up there?" Mami calls up from the deck, which makes them laugh all the more.

● ● ●

By the time they show up for breakfast next morning, Mami is wearing the ring. They try not to stare, but each time they look at each other, they can't help themselves. There are several giggle attacks during the waffle breakfast.

"How did you do it?" the girls ask Tía Lola once they've regrouped in their adjoining rooms. They are packing up their bathing suits and towels for today's camp outing: a morning trip to Lake Champlain, a picnic, then back in time for afternoon practice and the arrival of their guests from the city.

"I told her it was a mood ring that would help her sort out her feelings."

That's all it took? Mami didn't require any further explanation? But of course, Tía Lola has persuasive powers, even in the way she smiles!

Mami has agreed to wear the ring, so maybe if the stone turns violet or even blue (happy) or green (calm), she will realize she is really in love. Mami's monster will be slain, the Espadas can move to Vermont, and they can all get on with the rest of the summer, and whatever wonderful adventures Tía Lola has in store for them.

●●●

They drive out to Lake Champlain, the van packed with eight people, their swords, two large picnic baskets, and after some discussion, one dog. Mami says she can't bear the thought of leaving Valentino behind.

"So, what are you going to do when we leave Sunday?" That Essie is fearless! Miguel can't believe it: this girl has an even bigger mouth than Juanita. But he has to admit, he is going to miss Valentino—and baseball practice with Víctor—when the Espadas depart on Sunday.

"I supposed I'll die of heartbreak," Mami plays along.

"Well, we don't want to be responsible for murder," Essie goes on. "So either you move to Queens, or we have to move to Vermont." There it is, laid out, the choice Mami has to make. "And I don't think you'd like Queens. There's a lot of crime and drugs there." Essie is not sure of this fact, but she does know those are the first things parents worry about in a neighborhood. Crime and drugs.

Víctor looks in the rearview mirror and winks at his plucky daughter.

"What is this, a plot?" Mami asks, narrowing her eyes at Víctor suspiciously, but she is laughing.

"I love Vermont," Cari pipes up. "It's not scary like Queens."

"I love Vermont. I love Vermont." Her sisters take up the chant.

From way in back, Valentino agrees with a series of his own I-love-Vermont barks.

■■■

After a morning of swimming in Lake Champlain, they are starved. They find a picnic table and sit down, four on each side, Mami and Víctor together.

Victoria scoots in beside Mami so she can check on the you-know-what. But Mami's hands are so busy unpacking the picnic, opening containers, unwrapping sandwiches, Victoria is going to get a cramp in her neck trying to catch them at rest. Finally, Mami lays her left hand down on her napkin. She's wearing the mood ring on her *wedding-ring finger*! If that isn't significant, Victoria doesn't know what is.

"What color is it? What color is it???" Essie keeps mouthing from across the table.

Victoria is glancing all around for something the same color as the mood stone. Finally, she spots the green dish towel that was covering one of the picnic baskets. Very pointedly, she pats her mouth with it, until everyone is giggling.

Mami follows the gigglers' gaze. Victoria is suddenly aware that Mami's eyes are on her. Quickly, to disguise her signal, she wipes her whole face with the green dish towel. The gigglers explode into laughter.

By now, Mami is totally suspicious. "What is going on here?" she asks the whole table, but really she is looking at Víctor.

105

"Don't look at me." Víctor shrugs, laughing. He is as clueless as she is. But he's also very pleased to see that the kids are having such a good time together, something he hopes Linda is noticing.

"We're just really, really, really happy," Juanita says with emphasis. "Right, Miguel?"

As usual, his sister is going to blow everyone's cover with her heavy-handedness. But Mami especially is hanging on his next word, so Miguel has to agree that he's really, really, really happy, too. "I'm off the charts," he says smartly.

The girls roar with laughter, drowning out Valentino's barking.

●●●

They drive back through town to drop off Tía Lola and Juanita and the younger Swords at Colonel Charlebois'. They'll be riding their bikes home after another tea-and-cookies-and-stories visit.

What a shock when they stop in front of his house! A sign on the front lawn reads FOR RENT. Mami and Tía Lola clamber out of the van as soon as it stops moving. Has something happened to the colonel? Why else would his house be for rent? They press the buzzer over and over.

"What in tarnation?!" The colonel has swung open his door to find a mob of children, adults, and one barking dog, alarmed by the rental sign. "Of course I'm not going anywhere," he informs them. "I just got to thinking yesterday, after such fine company, that I don't want to be in this big old house by myself anymore. So I'm looking for a family to move in with me."

You could knock Essie over with a feather. "We'll take it," she wants to call out like someone at an auction, nervous to be outbid. She glances over at Papa with eyes that would rival Valentino's when he is in high begging mode at the dinner table.

Papa winks at her. "How many bedrooms do you have?" he asks Colonel Charlebois.

"How many do you need?" the old man comes right back at him.

Essie knows. She counted them yesterday. Besides the colonel's bedroom on the first floor, there are three more on the second floor and a bunch of little ones up in the attic. They could move into this house and each have a bedroom, even Valentino.

Mami listens quietly as Colonel Charlebois goes over all the details of the house. When it's time to leave, Víctor and Miguel walk back to the van, followed by Mami, who slips her arm affectionately around Victoria's waist. And in that moment, Juanita sees very clearly, the stone on the mood ring glows a really, really, really happy blue.

By the time the bikers arrive home, the car with New York plates is sitting in the driveway. Abuelito and Abuelita and Carmen are drinking lemonade on the back deck with Mami. Papi has already gone out to the back field to watch the tail end of the team's practice.

Juanita races into her grandparents' arms, exchanging *besitos* and *abrazos,* big kissy hugs. "We've been having camp all week," she begins. She's about to launch into a full report, but suddenly she remembers her manners. The two younger Swords have to be introduced to her grandparents. Carmen, of course, already knows the girls. She works with their father and is a family friend. In fact, the Swords call her Tía Carmen, even though she isn't technically their aunt.

The three girls all start talking at once about the exciting adventures of Tía Lola's summer camp. The visitors keep shaking their heads in disbelief. Could so much fun be packed into a single week?

When they're done with their summer camp report, Carmen notes, "Sounds like you girls are really loving Vermont." Cari and Essie nod vigorously.

"We really, really, really love Vermont," Cari elaborates. "We might even move here—if the ring turns violet, that means she loves Papa." Cari points to Mami.

Mami's face is a mixture of surprise and embarrassment. "So that's what's been going on! No wonder you kids keep staring at my ring like it's a crystal ball!" Now it's her turn to stare. Glancing down at her hand, Mami smiles at what she finds there.

●●●

After dinner, the girls retreat to Juanita's room to work on their posters for tomorrow's game. They can't be real cheerleaders, but they can hold up signs cheering on Charlie's Boys.

Miguel is on his way upstairs to get all his gear ready for early tomorrow morning. At eight sharp, Charlie's Boys will assemble at the town's baseball field, where the game will be held. Juanita's door opens. Essie peeks out and frantically gestures for Miguel to come in while the coast is clear.

"Cari blew it!" Essie tells him. She has already told Victoria. All their efforts have come to nothing.

"I didn't mean to." Cari is close to tears. Sometimes she just forgets something is a secret, and she'll tell because she loves to share.

"Maybe it's just as well," Victoria says, in part to make her little sister feel better. "Besides, I just finished helping your *mami* clear the dishes, and she's still wearing the ring. So even if she knows we're watching, she hasn't taken it off."

"Did you see what color it was?" Juanita asks. She has already reported that the stone turned blue over at Colonel Charlebois' house. From green (calm) to blue (happy) is progress.

"It was still blue," Victoria has to admit. "But like a really weird blue, the way the sky looks when there's going to be a rainbow." Rainbows are on her mind. For her poster, Victoria has drawn a huge one arcing over a field with a baseball flying way up above the scene. The poster reads HEY, CHARLIE'S BOYS, HIT THEM OVER THE RAINBOW!

"That is so cool," Essie says, momentarily distracted by one sister's masterpiece from the tragedy brought on by another sister's blabbing. "Mine is so blah." There it is again, the glass half full. Poor, pessimistic Essie. Growing up is not going to change her.

"I *love* your poster," Juanita protests. "It is *not* blah at all!" In fact, Essie's poster is the opposite of blah; it's downright bloody. KILL THE PANTHERS! it reads in big, bloody letters dripping into a sea of red. Essie will probably not be allowed to hold it up at the game. The coaches always give a little speech about good sportsmanship. Odd that Juanita should love Essie's gory poster, as hers is what Miguel would call lovey-dovey. A big, bold WE is printed at the top; CHARLIE'S BOYS, at the bottom. In the middle, Juanita has drawn a big red heart. All around the borders, Cari has been coloring little red hearts, as Juanita invited her to do a poster together.

There's a knock at the door that makes them all jump. Essie tiptoes over and cautiously cracks it open. "Oh, Tía Lola!" she cries in relief, letting her in.

Tía Lola has the look of someone with a secret to tell. "I come to report." Tía Lola holds out her right hand. Sitting in the center of her palm is Juanita's mood ring. "She took it off."

"But why?" Essie's voice is almost a wail.

"She said she already knows how she feels. She doesn't need a ring to tell her."

Miguel could say "I told you so." But right now, like the Swords, like his sister, all he wants to know is, what *is* Mami feeling?

"So????" Essie is already bracing herself for the worst.

Tía Lola shakes her head. "She wouldn't say how she feels."

The girls all groan. Even Miguel feels frustrated. Although he wasn't sold on the ring plan, he has gotten caught up in the girls' enthusiasm.

Just then there's another surprise knock on the door. The room goes absolutely still. "I know you're in there," Mami calls. "May I?" she asks, pushing open the door. In her hand is her sword, like she's come upstairs to cut off their heads for making so much noise.

"We were just, um, just finishing our posters, um," Victoria stammers, blinking furiously. She may as well take one of those markers and write LIAR across her forehead.

But Mami is too bent on her mission to notice. "Could I borrow the red marker, if you're finished?" she says, holding out her sword.

Victoria is relieved that's all Linda has come for. "Sure," she says, handing it over.

Essie, of course, is too curious to leave it at that. "What do you want it for?"

"To paint something on my sword."

"Like what?" Oh, Essie, give it up.

"Just some gore," Mami says happily. And then, seeing that they are all baffled, she adds, "You know, blood and gore like when you kill a monster." Mami waves her sword in the air. Then, just as mysteriously as she appeared, she disappears out the door.

Everyone is in bed early tonight. The newly arrived guests are exhausted after their long ride. Tomorrow will be a long and exciting day, especially for Miguel.

Perhaps that's why Mami comes upstairs to his room tonight. Miguel doesn't need tucking in, he's too old for that. But she has something special to tell him. "Whatever happens, *mi'jo,* my son, I want you to know I am so proud of you. You were such a good sport about the injury, so generous with Essie. And according to Víctor, you've come back playing better than ever. You're already a winner."

Miguel wishes he were good at expressing his feelings like Mami. But his mother seems to know how he feels just by looking in his eyes: I love you. I love Papi. I want you both to be happy.

Something about the way she leans in and kisses his forehead tells him she is happy. Something about the way she goes quietly out of the room, down the stairs, and wishes all the girls good night, blowing kisses to them that rise up through the heating vents and caress Miguel's sleepy face says that she is in love. Her mistake monster has been laid to rest. On her magic sword, she has painted not just blood and gore, but a big red heart, followed by the name Víctor.

Nine

saturday

Miguel's Big Game

Miguel wakes up this morning not knowing if he has truly woken up or if he is just getting out of bed after being awake all night. Seems like he didn't sleep a wink, playing baseball in his head instead. Not a good thing. Especially when he has to play a real game against the Panton Panthers today.

What he's hoping is that the excitement will carry him past the tiredness and he won't bottom out until after the bottom of the sixth. He dresses and heads down for breakfast, the house silent and steeped in sleep all around him.

Down in the kitchen, two people are already awake. Tía Lola and Víctor are both eager to know if Miguel's ready for the big game today.

Before they even ask, they can tell from the look on his face. Miguel has had a tough night, striking out, loading bases, dropping balls. It's like someone was making a video of all the baseball errors possible and hired Miguel to demonstrate.

"Come sit down, Captain." Víctor nods to the space beside him in the little alcove dining area in the kitchen. He seems to understand and doesn't push Miguel with a whole bunch of questions.

The sudden ring makes them all jump. Tía Lola races to grab the phone before a third ring wakes up the house. *"Buenos días, Owensito, ¿qué hay?"* In spite of himself, Miguel has to smile at the thought of Tía Lola wishing the tall teenager, "little Owen," a good morning and asking him what's up.

"Ay," Tía Lola sighs, and from the look on her face and the wail in her *"ay,"* Miguel knows this can't be good news. Sure enough, when he gets on the phone, Owen explains that Dean has been sick all night, some bug he caught, maybe from the colonel. Dean's definitely in no shape to play ball.

"I already talked to Rudy," Owen goes on. "He asked me to get in touch with you while he calls around to see who he can line up." Miguel knows what Coach Rudy is worried about. Patrick, their only sub for today's game, is their worst player, small for his age, intensely eager, but the muscle coordination just isn't there yet. Meanwhile, the team's losing its best player: Dean is a hard hitter and a great catcher with a strong arm—the kind of player who raises the bar for everyone on the team. It doesn't hurt that Dean is constantly practicing with his older brother. Owen, after all, is good enough to be helping Rudy coach. Miguel finds himself wishing that someone else will drop out and the game will have to be canceled. But he squelches the thought. What kind of an attitude is that for going into a game? He's defeated before he even starts.

Miguel is so distracted by the bad news, it's a quarter to eight by the time he glances up at the clock. The pregame warm-up starts in fifteen minutes! And where's Papi? Last night he said he wanted to drive Miguel to the town's baseball field, where the game is being held.

Miguel hurries into the den and shakes his father awake. "What? What?" Papi groans. Then he rolls over, muttering, "Five more minutes, *mi'jo*."

"Papi, I've got to go now!" Miguel knows five minutes, give or take, is no big deal. But with everything unraveling, he desperately wants to feel in control, even if it's over a minor detail. And his father has never been what Mami calls a morning person. Papi's five minutes could easily turn into fifteen or twenty before they're out the door. Another thought Miguel finds himself squelching: why can't his *papi* be more like Víctor?

Víctor comes up behind Miguel, keys in his hand. "Hey, Captain. I'll drop you off. Your father can catch up with you later."

Miguel hesitates. This will not go over well once Papi wakes up. But Miguel can't stop to worry about what could be. Everything's falling apart right now! "Okay," he finally says, collecting his gear.

Víctor's already down the front steps when who should

come bounding down the stairs but Essie, fully dressed in jeans and a T-shirt. "You're already going?" she asks.

Miguel nods, hoping to make a quick getaway. But he's forgetting what a piece of gum Essie can be. Of course she trots out after him and, when she sees her father in the van, asks if she can ride along.

Now it's Víctor hesitating. But the truth is that arguing with Essie can take time, and Miguel has to get going. "Fine with me," Miguel says, shrugging, since Víctor is looking at him to decide.

Most of his teammates have already arrived by the time they pull into the parking lot. The mood is grim. No team likes to lose its best player before an important game. Even Rudy looks uncharacteristically flustered.

Ironically, the one calm person is the messenger who delivered the bad news. Owen calls out the batting order, adding his two bits about the heroics of each player. When he gets to out-of-the-park Patrick (yeah, right!), Owen glances over at Rudy. Where to put Patrick so that he might do the least harm? One thing is sure, they can't risk making Patrick the catcher—it's too critical a position if they want to win this game.

Maybe it's the sight of Dean's folded uniform, which Owen brought along in case an unexpected sub should need it, or of Essie getting out of the van to say hi to her new pals, but Rudy's face takes on a studied look. "We're a summer-league team," he observes out of the blue. "And this young lady has practiced with us. Tell you what . . ." He points at Essie. "Are you ready to play ball?"

Miguel is about to scream "NO!" But Essie beats him

to it with her shout of "YES!" Miguel can't believe this is happening! This is worse than his bad dreams last night. But he reasons with himself. He wants to beat the Panton Panthers, doesn't he? This might be the only way. He has watched Essie at practice, and though she can be a pessimist and a pest, one thing you can't take away from her is the girl can play baseball.

Dean's uniform is, of course, too big on Essie. Before you know it, Víctor has made an emergency run to the house and come back with Tía Lola and her sewing kit. While the team warms up, Tía Lola gets to work hemming the legs and sleeves. A half hour later when Essie emerges from the dugout, she looks like a smaller version of Dean. As she and Miguel warm up, getting into a rhythm, pitching, catching, working out their signals, Miguel can't help feeling that the team got lucky finding Essie to replace Dean.

When they break after warming up, the tension also seems to have broken. The team's fighting spirit is finally kicking in. "You're looking good, nice catches, excellent throwing, scorcher hits." Rudy has something good to say to each player. They all perk up with the praise.

Except for Patrick, who sits at the end of the bench, his gaze cast down as if he's ashamed of himself. The team tries to make it up to him, including him in jokes, praising his improved catching and batting. But the only way to reverse the sad look on the boy's face is to let him play in the game today.

The Panton team arrives. Twelve hefty teens emerge from a van with a crouching panther painted on its side. A team with its own van! These guys are serious ballplayers, not just boys in search of summer fun. Furthermore, they don't look like eleven- and twelve-year-olds. Some of these guys must already be shaving! The rules for these summer-league games are a little loose, since towns and teams don't have to follow the official Little League handbook. Look at Essie, she'd never be able to play if this were a regular game. But the age-limit rule is usually observed.

"All that glitters is not gold." Tía Lola has sat down beside Miguel where he's sizing up the opposition. "Good things come in small packages," she adds, using another of the sayings she has learned and nodding toward Essie. "You have a chance to win this game, Miguel. But you have to convince yourself or you have already lost." Then Tía Lola adds a saying that Miguel hasn't heard before. "Don't dig your grave with your own knife and fork."

Miguel has to smile. Tía Lola has a way of saying just the right thing at the right moment. "I know," he agrees with his aunt. "I just didn't sleep a whole lot last night. Worrying, I guess, about everything."

Tía Lola nods as if she already knows Miguel's laundry list of worries: his concern about betraying his father if he likes Víctor, disappointing his mother if he doesn't; hurting his father if he doesn't like Carmen, or his mother if he does. It's as if, overnight, Miguel's whole life has turned into some crazy game, and he doesn't even understand the rules, so how's he supposed to know how to behave? Furthermore, how can he concentrate on baseball when he has gotten all tangled up in this other game?

"Nobody is keeping score in the game that really

counts," Tía Lola says, as if she can read his mind. Miguel must look confused as to what game his aunt is talking about, because she goes on to explain, *"El juego de la vida."*

The game of life? Miguel sighs. He's no philosopher. And this is no time to get in over his head in deep thoughts.

"This game of life is really very simple," Tía Lola goes on. "There is only one very important rule to follow." Tía Lola whips out her sword and gives it to Miguel to hold. It's only now that Miguel realizes that in his daze this morning, he forgot to pick up his own sword as he left his room. Another strike against him on this tricky day.

Miguel wonders what kind of a rule requires that you hold a sword in order to hear it. "So what's the rule, Tía Lola?"

"Okay, ready, set, go!" Tía Lola jokes. Miguel hates to tell his aunt, but she is in a whole other sport. "This very hard rule is: no matter what you do, you have to try to be happy doing it. First, if you're happy, you take yourself off the list of people Tía Lola has to help. Second, if you're happy doing something, you'll have fun no matter the result. Let's see. What number are we at?" Tía Lola looks down at her fingers, scowling.

Miguel shakes his head, smiling fondly at his crazy aunt. "You're at strike two, Tía Lola," he jokes.

"Okay, here's the home run," Tía Lola says. She's mixing up baseball plays, but at least she is back in the game. "If you are happy, the people who love you will be happy, too."

Miguel doesn't get it. How can being happy be a hard

rule? But Tía Lola has a point. Seems like everyone in the world wants to be happy, but the world is not a happy place. "So what's the sword for?"

"To remind you!" Tía Lola grins.

Almost as if to test Miguel's ability to follow this hard rule of being happy in real time, his family arrives. Miguel has been dreading meeting up with Papi. His father is bound to be upset about Víctor driving Miguel to the ballpark this morning. For a brief moment, Miguel considers hurrying into the dugout so he doesn't have to face Papi right before the big game. But call it magic, call it the rule of gold, before Miguel knows it, he's waving hello with Tía Lola's sword.

His father trots over, a rolled-up bundle under his arm. "Thank you, *mi'jo,* for not being upset with your old man. I'm really sorry about this morning. I guess with all this country quiet, I just slept through my alarm." Papi unfolds the banner he painted on a long canvas sheet. "My peace offering," he calls it. It's a beautiful green field of dreams, so eye-catching that even a couple of players from the Panton team come over to check it out.

His *papi* is an artist, not an athlete; Miguel has always known that. But it's only at this moment that Miguel realizes that Papi has his own way of celebrating his son with the talent that he does have.

And right now, Miguel has a talent he wants to use—playing ball. If he loses, he loses. He can always try again. Tomorrow will be another day, and it ain't over till it's over, as Yogi Berra used to say. It's funny how Tía Lola often reminds Miguel of this old-time baseball great.

●●●

This particular game between the Panton Panthers and Charlie's Boys is going to go down in local baseball history as one that kept the fans on the edge of their seats until the very end. The score inches up—first the Panton Panthers are ahead by one run, then Charlie's Boys, neck and neck. At one point, Miguel looks up and realizes he's got a whole cheering section, posters pumping up and down, Papi's banner unfolded, Victoria whistling, a bunch of swords waving. It can't help but boost his confidence and flood his heart with gratitude. All these people are rooting for him—and not just in today's game. Tía Lola is right. They want to see him happy each and every day of his life.

What really allows Charlie's Boys to stay right in there with the Panthers is Essie's amazing ability to slam them out of the ballpark. The Panther pitcher can't seem to throw her a ball she can't hit. Each time she swings, folks in the bleachers stand up to see where it's going to land. It's as if Essie has taken her older sister's poster to heart: HIT THEM OVER THE RAINBOW! And she does.

The crowd is hoarse from shouting. And it isn't going to get quieter now at the top of the fifth with the game tied, 3–3. Coach Rudy gathers them in a huddle. It's time for substitutions, if there are going to be any. Unbelievably, Rudy announces that he's taking Essie out and putting in Patrick. This is suicide! Miguel can understand letting Patrick play, but put him out of the way in right field. Don't make him the catcher and risk a weak player in a key position at this point in the game.

But later, at the barbecue at Miguel's house, Rudy will explain. "I wanted to win this big game so much for the team, I forgot what playing baseball is all about. I did wrong bypassing Patrick and picking Essie to replace Dean. But God, who loves us as much as some of us love baseball, gave me a second chance to do the right thing. He hit me over the head with his wake-up bat!"

But here at the top of the fifth inning, God hasn't hit Miguel with the same wake-up bat. He pulls his coach over. "Please, don't take Essie out now, please." But Rudy is sticking to what he knows is right. "This goes, Captain."

Miguel feels like staging a mutiny. After all, he is the captain, and like Tía Lola always says, *Donde manda capitán no manda soldado.* Where the captain is in charge, the soldier can't give orders. But Rudy isn't any old foot soldier, he's the coach, and in baseball that means he's the boss. So Miguel tries another suggestion. As the two outsiders, Essie and Patrick have been practicing on the sidelines all week. They'll make a more decent pairing than Miguel and Patrick will. "Okay, Coach, then bring Essie in for me."

Rudy's eyebrows lift in surprise. Miguel is not a kid who easily steps out of a baseball game. Look at the way he persisted after bruising that ankle. But Rudy must realize that he's not the only one getting a second chance to be a bigger person today. Coach and captain lock eyes. "Ankle still a little sore?" Rudy is offering Miguel a way to explain himself to his teammates. Miguel nods. Although it will be two innings before the game is over, this is how you really win in life as well as in baseball.

"It's the little victories in a game that count," Rudy has always told them. But this time they get to have both. Essie's fastball strikes out two Panthers, and the last out is recorded when Andrew snags a line drive. Meanwhile, batting at the bottom of the final inning of the game, little Patrick whams one up, up, and away: a fly ball that surprises even the Panthers' right fielder, who stumbles and drops the ball. Essie makes it home, and Charlie's Boys have won the game, 4–3, and are they ever happy about it!

● ● ●

"Thanks for letting me pitch, Captain," Essie tells Miguel at the team barbecue after the game. "Hey, you were right. You really can work magic."

What on earth is she talking about? She's the one with the magic arm, fastballs that strike out batters, and home runs that travel for miles. "What magic?"

"Remember how I said if you could work magic, you'd make this week more fun than Disney World? Well, it's been like ten times more fun!" Essie is still on a high after winning the game today. Maybe she'll never come down again.

When they're almost done with eating, Rudy clinks his glass. He has an announcement to make. "The time has come. Your old coach just can't keep up with you young folks. This is going to have to be my last season coaching."

The team's spirit takes a collective nosedive. Good thing Rudy made this announcement after the game, not before.

They would have lost the game for sure. But Rudy shakes his head. "The magic is in you guys, not in me." He sure sounds a lot like Tía Lola. "And hey, buddies, I'm not leaving you out there without a paddle. I've got a plan." He lets them all hang in suspense a moment before nodding toward Víctor. "This last week, I've been watching you, Vic. You've got what it takes to coach these kids and bring out the best in the team. I'm sure hoping you'll soon be moving up here so you can take over."

Víctor has been looking wistfully at Linda during Rudy's passing-of-the-bat speech. After an awkward silence, he gives the same reply he has been giving his girls: "It's not just up to me, you know."

"Well, if it's up to the team, all in favor, say aye." Rudy turns to the young players he has been coaching for several seasons now. They all cheer for Coach Víctor.

All but their captain, who is feeling torn. Miguel would love to have Víctor coach the team. But Papi is looking on. Before he votes, Miguel wants to be sure that his father knows that in the big game of life, as Tía Lola calls it, Papi will always be Miguel's head coach.

●●●

"I'm glad you've been having such a good time, *mi'jo,*" his father says, his voice a little sad. Finally, father and son are getting a chance to walk out to the back pasture together after the barbecue. Once it's dark, Miguel's family and the Swords will have a farewell campfire together, Tía Lola's idea.

Miguel has been telling Papi all about his adventures this week. How Tía Lola started a camp for the girls, but then that camp fizzled out, and the whole place turned into one big camp for everybody. The nighttime treasure hunt, the magic swords to help them with some challenge, the last-minute Fourth of July party. Even though he hurt his ankle and couldn't play baseball for a couple of days, Miguel has to agree with Essie. It has been a fun week.

Only one thing has been missing: Papi. Miguel wants his father to know this. But unlike Mami or Juanita or Tía Lola, Miguel doesn't find it easy putting his feelings into words. And right this moment, he doesn't have Tía Lola's or his sword to help him—both are up in his room.

But Tía Lola keeps saying that the magic is really inside each and every person, and the swords just remind you of that fact. So Miguel takes a deep breath and blurts it all out in one sentence: "Papi, no matter what, you'll always be my father, even if Mami marries Víctor, right?"

"Of course, *mi'jo!*" Papi says, grabbing his son in a long, lingering hug. When he pulls away, Papi's eyes are teary, the happy kind of tears. "I want your mother to be happy. And if she's happy and I'm happy, I think you and Juanita will be happy, too. And sure, there might be moments that I feel a little sad that I'm not the one here living with you. But when I get to missing you too much, I'll jump in the car with Car or ask your *mami* to send you and Juanita down with your Tía Lola. Deal?"

More than a deal! It's exactly what Miguel wants, to see his father often and still get to live in Vermont.

All this talking about Tía Lola reminds Miguel how

much his aunt helped him today. So why not give Tía Lola his sword now that he has hers? The golden rule of giving: give unto others as they have given unto you!

Upstairs, Miguel finds his sword still propped on the chair by his bedroom door, where he put it so he'd remember to take it with him to the game today. Before taking it down to the campfire, Miguel crosses out his name and writes Tía Lola's on the blade, followed by a big smiley face.

saturday night and sunday morning

The Departure of the Swords

"Tonight, we say *hasta luego*," Tía Lola tells the assembled group. "Farewell for now, but not forever."

They are sitting around a big campfire in the backyard. Night has fallen, a dark one with an overcast sky. Abuelito and Abuelita have gone to bed, tired after a packed day. But everyone else lingers, not wanting to break the magic of being together.

The three Espada girls sit in ascending age order, followed by Carmen and Papi, Miguel and Juanita, then Valentino, Mami with her arm around him, and finally Víctor, closing the circle. In the center stands Tía Lola, feeding the fire. With the flames lighting up her face and shadows springing from her arms as she gestures, she looks like the wise woman in a fairy tale.

"Some of you have been here a week, and some of you just arrived. But tonight, we all join a circle of friendship that we can always come back to in our hearts."

"Oh, Tía Lola," Victoria says, her eyes shining brightly. "You're going to make us all cry."

"I'm not going to cry," Essie declares, clearing her throat, just in case. Sobs have been known to sneak up on her the back way.

Cari snuggles close to her father. "I don't want to leave Vermont, Papa," she sniffles.

"Well, we have to!" Essie says sharply. Of course, she'd like to give herself the luxury of wishing otherwise. But despite her tough facade, tiny drops accumulate in the corners of her eyes.

Victoria is still hoping her father, or actually Linda, will make an announcement. But Linda hasn't said anything, and by now, it's unlikely she will. The move will have to be put on hold. Why must adults always put brakes on their feelings? No wonder Romeo and Juliet were teenagers! Of course, they had to die before they grew up and ruined everything! "I'm going to miss everybody, that's for sure." Although "everybody" includes all of Victoria's new Vermont friends around this circle, one particular face pops up in her head. A tall, blue-eyed fourteen-year-old with beautiful dark brown hair. "It's sad when things have to end."

Across the circle, Valentino lets out one of his all-purpose sighs.

"I know goodbyes are difficult," Tía Lola allows, "but without them, we can't start a new adventure."

Essie likes the sound of that. A new adventure. Before this week of summer camp, she thought of her life as just her boring life. But Tía Lola has made her realize that each day is a story that Essie can try to end happily. And happiness is no longer confined to places like Disney World. Happiness can happen anywhere, even in Queens, though Essie would prefer having her happy adventures in Vermont from now on.

She grips her samurai sword. It's curious how, around the circle, everyone has brought their swords along, even though Tía Lola didn't suggest they do so. It just seemed appropriate to bring them to this closing campfire. Except for the memories in their heads and one lame mood ring, the swords are their only souvenir from this week at Tía Lola's summer camp.

"The first night you were with us"—Tía Lola nods toward the arc of Espadas forming one part of the circle— "you went on a treasure hunt, remember?" Of course they remember! Fond smiles spread across the girls' faces. "So now, as we close, we are going to have another kind of treasure adventure."

"Cool!" Essie is on her feet, ready to go. And they better move it. Rain is headed their way. She has been hearing the rumbles of thunder. Any minute now, Papa's going to suggest they go indoors before they all get struck by lightning or catch their death of cold.

But strangely, Papa says nothing, as if he, too, is under

the spell of Tía Lola's voice. The fire crackles. Far off, the bullfrogs are serenading the Swords goodbye. *Day is done, gone the Swords, from the lakes, from the hills, from Vermont. . . .*

"Shouldn't we go get our flashlights, Tía Lola?" Essie asks. How else to navigate their way on this dark night without a star or sliver of moon in the sky?

"It isn't that kind of a treasure hunt, Esperanza," Tía Lola explains, using her musical name. Each time Tía Lola says it, another ray of sunshine works its way into Esperanza's once-upon-a-time-gloomy heart. No more! She is full of high hopes for her storybook life. "This treasure adventure takes place in our imagination." Tía Lola taps her head, and the swing of her arm makes a great, shadowy wing flap around the circle.

Essie groans and sits back down. What's a treasure hunt without a search for clues and a lot of running around? But Essie doesn't despair, because if she has learned one thing this week, it's that Tía Lola can turn anything into fun.

"Here's how it works. Listen well. A word to the wise is *suficiente!*" Tía Lola has been learning so many sayings in English this summer. By fall, she is going to be a wise woman in two languages. "I want each of you to think of something *especial* from this week that you'd like everyone to have."

The silence around the circle reminds Miguel of English class after Mrs. Prouty gave them one of her hard assignments. The difference is that his aunt is always good about explaining things. But before she can, Essie is already asking, "So how exactly is this a treasure hunt, Tía Lola?"

"A treasure *adventure*. We are not hunting treasure, Esperanza, we're actually filling up the chest"—Tía Lola taps her chest—"with treasures that we can reach in and use when we need them. All we will have to do is think back on tonight."

Essie nods several deep, all-knowing nods, like now she gets it. Maybe that's why Tía Lola asks her if she would like to start. Uncharacteristically, Essie, who always likes to be first, says she'll pass for now.

"Can we participate?" Carmen asks, nodding toward Papi. "I mean, we haven't been here all week. But I've gotten so much just in one day. I'd like to give something back to the treasure chest."

"Of course you can participate!" Tía Lola says. "Any contribution means there's more treasure in our chest. But first, before you put your treasure into words, everybody should close their eyes."

"How come?" Cari wants to know. She isn't sure she wants to close her eyes. It's already dark and scary enough.

"Because the treasure is imaginary, so you have to picture it. And once you do, it's inside you," Tía Lola explains. "Like when you are dreaming in the day."

"You mean daydreaming?" Cari likes for words to be just right.

"Exactly!" Tía Lola claps her hands.

Cari closes her eyes, and surprisingly, it's not scary at all. Like a theater with the lights off and a fun, unscary movie about to start.

"Cierren los ojos," Tía Lola reminds the others. They all close their eyes, presumably also Tía Lola, but who can tell with their eyes closed?

"Okay, here's what I'd like to put in our imaginary treasure chest," Carmen begins. "A huge bag of gratitude. I hope that's the kind of treasure you mean, Tía Lola?" Carmen cracks open her eyes and sees Tía Lola at the center of the circle, her eyes closed, smiling. "I feel so grateful," Carmen continues, "grateful to Linda for letting us all stay under one roof, grateful to Tía Lola for sharing her room, grateful to Miguel and Esperanza for playing such an exciting baseball game, grateful to Juanita for her beautiful flowers. . . ."

Miguel feels a few drops on his face. Carmen sounds sincerely grateful. But somebody better cut her off, or the treasure chest is going to end up as a rain bucket.

"I feel so grateful to be a part of two wonderful families—my friend Víctor's family and Daniel's. And Linda's," Carmen adds, wanting to compliment everybody. "Anytime anyone needs a little gratitude, just reach inside our treasure chest."

"¡Perfecto!" Tía Lola says, complimenting Carmen for her perfect contribution.

Victoria has been making her own mental list of things she is grateful for. But without a certain addition, most of the things on her list cancel out. "I have something to add to our treasure chest, if I can go next," Victoria offers. It's something she has learned this week that she really needs now in her life. She takes a deep, brave breath and plunges ahead. "I'd like to put in independence."

Victoria senses her father's sadness traveling around the circle. Oh, Papa, she feels like saying, please, please, please, let me go! I promise I'll always come back again. "If you don't have independence, how can you follow your dreams?" Victoria is addressing the whole group, but she is really talking to her father. "Say you want to study Spanish in Mexico or move to Vermont to live in nature . . ." Her voice drifts off. She's not ready to share another aspect of being independent: having a boyfriend. Her father would go ballistic.

"You need independence to become who you are." Linda helps her out. "I would never be where I am today without it."

"You said it!" Carmen agrees. "I used every ounce of independence I had to go to law school. That's why I'm so grateful you are putting some in our chest, Victoria. I definitely need a refill."

Víctor can't deny the truth of these testimonies. He is a lawyer, after all. "If you're ready for more, Tía Lola . . ." In the silence, the fire—or Tía Lola—whispers, *"Sí, sí, sí,"* giving Víctor the go-ahead.

Miguel braces himself. If Víctor mentions love or marriage, will that change the warm, wonderful mood of this circle?

"I choose dreams," Víctor says dreamily. Miguel isn't too surprised, given how Víctor helped him achieve his dream of playing in today's game. "We should never let go of them, whatever they may be, whether it's playing baseball or being an artist"—nice of him to include this for Papi's benefit—"or marrying the one you love. Dreams are our life's blood. So, I am going to put a big hunk of this wish in our treasure chest, Tía Lola!"

"There's room for it," Tía Lola says, laughing. That is

the nice thing about the imagination. It's expandable, reversible, flexible, durable, etc., etc., etc.

Juanita has been trying really hard to picture each person's contribution. It hasn't been easy. What are you supposed to picture for gratitude or independence or dreams? But Tía Lola did say you could pick something you loved from this week's summer camp to contribute to the chest. "I want to put in flowers, magical flowers that bloom all year round."

From the silence that greets her announcement, Juanita wonders if she didn't play this game right. She can hear her brother's voice in her head, just like the first night of the Swords' arrival, when Juanita tore the clue at the treasure hunt. Miguel didn't call her stupid out loud, but she could see it written all over his face. Now, with her eyes closed, she can't read his expression, but she can sense what he is thinking: That's a stupid treasure! "Are flowers okay?" Juanita asks Tía Lola. She is ready to argue her case, something she has learned this week from Essie and her sisters. Flowers should be allowed! For one thing, they are a lot easier to picture than anything else anyone has said so far.

"I think flowers are something we can all use more of," Tía Lola approves wholeheartedly. "They remind us that even the most amazing feat begins with a little seed of effort, watered with a whole lot of patience and practice."

Juanita knows Miguel didn't actually say anything against her flower treasure. But she feels like turning to her brother and saying, "So there!"

Now that Juanita has chosen flowers, Cari wants to add something she loves from nature as well. "Can I put in tadpoles? Also, their mothers and fathers," she adds. After all, Cari would not want any treasure that involved making orphans, even if they're just frogs.

This is getting a little silly, Miguel is thinking. By now, he understands how this adventure works. The treasure chest is for special feelings or things you learned this week. But Tía Lola being Tía Lola, she has a way of turning even a ridiculous contribution into something worthwhile.

"I think tadpoles and frogs together are a great addition for our imaginary treasure chest," Tía Lola tells Cari. "And we don't even have to take the real ones out of their pond."

"But wait a minute." Essie is back to her contrary self. "How are frogs and tadpoles supposed to be treasure?"

"Because!" Cari snaps right back. She has learned to be brave and bold this week. The two sisters have opened their eyes and are glaring at each other, which is against the rules of this treasure adventure.

"Girls," their father reminds them.

"Close your eyes," Tía Lola says more gently. "Imagine those necklaces of eggs, how they turn into tadpoles, how the tadpoles turn into frogs. . . . This is very valuable treasure. Our lives are full of changes. And at each stage, we get to be a whole new person, but with our old selves still inside us."

Cari's chest swells with pride. She doesn't totally understand what Tía Lola means, but she has been vindicated.

"Thank you for your treasure, Cari." It's Miguel's father speaking up now. "I, of all people around this circle, have definitely been through many changes. I hope for the better."

Mami doesn't say anything. But when Miguel cracks open his eyes, he catches a glimpse of Carmen touching Papi's knee, as if she certainly agrees.

"What I'd like to put in the circle is second chances. So if we make a mistake, we can get the opportunity to try again and do better."

A different kind of silence now travels around the circle. As if Papi were speaking directly to Mami through his addition to the treasure chest. And Mami would be the first to admit that everybody makes mistakes. She's always telling Miguel to just pick himself up and try again.

Mami clears her throat so everyone knows she wants to speak up next. "Forgiveness," she says, plain and simple. "I think it's important to forgive so you can move on with an open heart." She doesn't offer any further explanation. Maybe Miguel is imagining it, but he hears the fire whispering, *Yes, yes, yes.*

He is about to take his turn when Esperanza speaks up. "Friendship. I want to put in friendship. That's what's made me love Vermont most of all."

"I love Vermont," her little sister agrees, mending the rift between them.

"Friendship is a wonderful addition," Tía Lola says. "Without it, the world is a lonely place."

For some reason, Colonel Charlebois pops into Essie's head. She wonders if he has found some renters so he doesn't have to be so lonely in his big, empty house. If only her family could move in! But it doesn't look like this will be happening. Neither Papa nor Linda has said a word about future plans. Essie is going to have to reach into that chest, even before she leaves Vermont, in order to *forgive* them both for disappointing her.

Valentino barks, reminding everyone that he, too, is a part of this circle. But unlike them, he can only express himself with tail wags, sighs, barks. Maybe that is his addition to the treasure chest: company that doesn't need to use words. You can sit quietly around a campfire with friends and feel totally happy.

"Okay, Tía Lola." Miguel takes the final turn. "What I want to put in is also a present for you, okay?"

Now it's Tía Lola breaking her own rule, opening her eyes. "*¿Para mi?*" She is surprised that her nephew came prepared with a gift *for her* when he didn't even know about this treasure adventure she thought up for their last night together.

"Yes, for you," Miguel says, picking up his sword. By now they have all opened their eyes so that they can see what the gift for Tía Lola might be. Miguel hopes his aunt won't be too disappointed that he's just giving back something she gave him. "I want you to have my sword. See, it says 'Tía Lola,' and the smiley face is for happiness. That's what I want to put in the treasure chest, happiness, with a big chunk of it for you to keep for yourself."

A wide smile spreads across Tía Lola's face. In fact, she looks like the model for the big smiley face on her new sword. "*¡Gracias!*" she says, accepting the gift from her nephew.

Seconds later, as if it, too, has been waiting to say *gracias,* the sky lets loose its splashy gratitude. The rain pours down, sending a whole circle of happy campers scurrying indoors.

The garden gratefully soaks it in. Everyone makes a dash for the house, leaving their swords behind. What does it matter anymore? The swords have served their purpose. Meanwhile, the treasure chest is full, mostly with what everyone learned and loved this week of Tía Lola's summer camp.

Only Essie runs back, to retrieve her samurai sword. It is so thoroughly soaked, she leaves it unsheathed in the mudroom overnight so that the blade and scabbard can dry off. In the morning, when she checks them before breakfast, the sword is dry, but the scabbard is still damp inside.

Brunch is a hectic affair, everyone's luggage lying around as if they were in an airport, but with none of the excitement of a plane trip in the offing. Only a long, boring car ride back to the city. The kids feel glum. The rain doesn't help. At one point when Essie glances out the back window of the house, the campfire looks like a tiny pond surrounded by seven cast-off Excaliburs. Papa seems sad, and Linda unusually subdued, though with all the commotion of parting, it's hard to tell for sure.

Right after brunch, Papi and Carmen and Abuelito and Abuelita depart. Soon it's the Swords in the mudroom, packing up for their trip home. In the kitchen, Mami and Tía Lola are preparing a basket with snacks for them to take. Papa has pulled the van up on the lawn so he can load the back with their suitcases and backpacks without getting too wet. He works grimly, as if he were sealing up the entrance to his heart with each piece of luggage he stuffs inside.

When everything else is packed, Essie checks again, but

the scabbard is still not dry. "Can I take it home like this?" she asks her father tentatively, holding up the sword in one hand and the scabbard in the other. "I'll be careful, promise." She knows how strict Papa can be about dangerous objects that might slice off toes or stab a dog in the guts.

But Papa doesn't seem to care one way or the other. This is both welcome (Essie can get away with murder!) and disconcerting (who's covering her back if not her father?).

"What's the problem?" Mami wants to know. She and Tía Lola have just entered with a large basket of goodies covered with a green dish towel. Both are smiling happily, as if the Swords were just arriving rather than getting ready to go.

"It's not really a problem," Essie is quick to explain before the nonproblem becomes a problem. "Just that the sword's scabbard is still damp from last night, but I can just wrap it in a towel for the ride home."

Mami crouches down beside her. "Here's an alternate plan, okay? Rather than taking it down to bring it right back up, why not just keep it here for when you move to Vermont real soon? Don't you think so, Víctor?"

It's as if a bucket of happiness has just splashed on Papa's face. Essie is the first to notice. "You mean, we *are* going to move to Vermont?" Essie's father looks toward Mami, wanting confirmation.

"I meant for it to be more of a surprise." Mami is blushing with sudden self-consciousness. She reaches under the dish towel and pulls out a note from the basket and hands it to Víctor. " 'To all the Swords,' " he reads out loud.

" 'Please move to Vermont and bring Valentino with you, or I will die of a broken heart, and you will be responsible for murder.' "

The girls break out in cheers. Valentino barks and wags his tail. Mami has said *yes!* Papa gives her a long, happy hug. But his happiness is too great to keep to just the two of them. He hugs each of his daughters, then Juanita and Tía Lola, and finally Miguel. With his hair wet and messed up, he could be a young man again, getting a second chance to live out a new dream. Meanwhile, Essie seems to have forgotten all about her samurai sword. She can live with several weeks of not getting anything she wants if at the end of this sacrifice she will get to move to Vermont.

Plans will be made over the phone in the days and weeks to come. But for now, it's time to say goodbye. Difficult as parting is, it's certainly a lot easier when you know you're coming back soon. Mami and Juanita step out onto the porch to wave until the van disappears around the bend in the driveway.

Miguel hangs back in the mudroom, dazed by the news he has just heard. Then, as if a whole week has not passed, his aunt is standing beside him. She squeezes his shoulder, just as she did upon the Swords' arrival. Reach into our treasure chest, her gaze is reminding him. Find what you need!

Miguel thinks back on last night's campfire. He is grateful that his parents have reconciled. That they are both happy. That soon his team will have a great new coach. Still, big changes lie ahead. But Miguel will have Cari's tadpoles and Victoria's independence to help him, plus three new friends, even if they are all girls. Most of all, Tía Lola will be beside him, as she is now, reminding him to keep reaching deeper, past flowers and tadpoles, second chances, forgiveness, friendship, gratitude, independence, until he finds his very own happiness.

acknowledgments

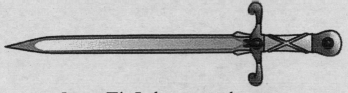

Just as Tía Lola gave each camper
a magical sword,
I am awarding
each of you
who helped me write this book
a special sword
to help you
slay monsters,
cut flowers,
achieve your dreams,
and much, much more.

Also and always,
my thanks and *gracias*
to la Virgencita de la Altagracia.
Swords go to: Brad Nadeau, Weybridge Elementary
School, Weybridge 2009 Little League team, Coach
Charlie Messenger, Roberto Veguez, Erica Stahler,
Lyn Tavares, Susan Bergholz, Erin Clarke,
Bill Eichner

Turn the page for a sneak peek at
Tía Lola's next *aventura:*
How Tía Lola Ended Up Starting Over

chapter one

How Tía Lola Saved the Swords from Starvation

Tía Lola and the children are having an emergency meeting in the big attic room in Colonel Charlebois's house. They are all brainstorming about how the Swords are going to survive now that they have moved to Vermont.

Miguel and Juanita can't help thinking about their own move here a year and nine months ago. Their parents were separating. Miguel and Juanita were leaving all their friends and their *papi* behind in New York City to come to this strange place. But at least Mami had a job. And they didn't have to be all alone in the house while she worked long hours. A few weeks after their move, their aunt from the Dominican Republic, Tía Lola, came to visit and decided to stay.

"Don't worry, Swords," Juanita says, brandishing a pretend sword, as if she were leading a charge. Swords is a fun nickname for the Espadas, whose last name means "sword" in Spanish.

"But we haven't come up with a way to earn some money," Essie wails. She is the middle Sword, the one who is usually full of ideas *and,* her father likes to add, full of *diablitos.* Whenever Papa wants to say something rude or cussy, he says it in Spanish. Like saying *"diablitos"* makes it okay to call your daughter a little devil! "I mean, Papa hasn't found a job, and our savings aren't going to last forever. If something doesn't happen soon, we're going to starve."

"I don't want to starve," little Cari sniffles. She is the youngest of the three Espadas and scares easily.

Valentino, the Espadas' golden Lab, lifts his head and sighs worriedly. If the family is going to starve, he will be the first to feel the rationing.

"Essie, you're not being helpful," Victoria scolds. As the eldest, she is always putting out the fires her middle sister starts. It's like Essie specializes in worst-case scenarios. If she could only find a job as a worst-case scenario consultant, the family would be millionaires.

"We, your *amigos* and *amigas,* will not let you starve!" Tía Lola assures them. She nods toward Miguel and Juanita. "And remember, your friend Rudy will always welcome you at his restaurant." Rudy owns the wildly popular Amigos Café in town. Tía Lola has helped out so many times on busy nights, Rudy has said that whenever she or her friends want a meal, it's on the house.

But Victoria knows her father would never accept a free meal. "Papa would think it was charity."

"So we go by ourselves." Essie lifts her chin defiantly.

"And let Papa starve?" In Cari's sweet, young voice, this does not sound okay, even to Essie.

"No one is going to starve," Tía Lola repeats. *"Se lo prometo!"*

"I promise, too." Juanita raises her right hand. "Me, Tía Lola, and Miguel do solemnly pledge that we will never ever let the Swords starve." Juanita is hoping to inject some humor into the grim gathering, but nobody laughs. "I'll bring you food from our house," she adds, more to the point.

"Especially all her vegetables," Miguel jokes.

Juanita scowls at her brother. Miguel has been in sixth grade only a week, and he's already such a know-it-all.

"Okay, people, let's try really, really hard," Victoria says, stepping in again to avoid sparks. Now that her father is dating Miguel and Juanita's mother, Victoria is being kept busy putting out fires in *both* families. "I'm sure that we can figure out a way to earn tons of money."

Silence greets this hopeful pronouncement. Even Tía Lola is looking frustrated. The beauty mark above her right eye is lost in her wrinkled brow.

"There's *sooooo* much talent in this room!" Victoria is beginning to sound desperate, even to her own ears. Like a cheerleader for a team that has never won a game and never will.

Essie's face suddenly brightens. She is remembering the genuine samurai sword Colonel Charlebois gave her this past summer. "I could give sword-fighting lessons."

"Way to go, Essie!" Victoria says, trying to sound enthusiastic. But she doubts that sword-fighting lessons will be in big demand in a small town in Vermont. Still, it's important to encourage Essie those rare times when she is being positive. Victoria writes down "sword fighting?" on the SOS list on her clipboard.

"And baseball lessons," Essie continues, now positively on a roll. An awesome pitcher and a home-run hitter, Essie is always looking for someone to practice with—and a few of Miguel's teammates have taken her up on it. So maybe she should charge for her time. "You want to help me, Miguel?"

Miguel doesn't like the idea of charging his friends, but he can't come up with any other way to help. Given that Víctor, the Swords' father, might someday marry his mother, it's too bad that no one in their combined families has a lot of money. His own father, Papi, is an artist whose day job—decorating department store windows down in New York City—is not a big moneymaker. Papi's fiancée, Carmen, is a lawyer, but like Víctor, who worked in the same firm up till a month ago, Carmen does a lot of free work. So what the right hand earns, the left hand gives away.

The only rich person they all know is Colonel Charlebois, who has been super generous with both families. In fact, neither family would have a roof over its head if it weren't for him. It was Colonel Charlebois who rented his old farmhouse to Miguel and Juanita and Mami when they first moved to Vermont. Then, when the colonel learned Mami was looking for their very own house to buy, he very generously turned the rent payments into house payments. The farmhouse on ten acres is on its way to becoming theirs.

Now the colonel has taken in the Espadas, though he claims it has nothing to do with helping them. Even before the Espadas decided to move to Vermont, the colonel had made up his mind to share his big house in town with housemates. He was too lonely living by himself, after spending his whole life surrounded by hundreds and thousands of soldiers in the army.

But so far, the colonel has refused any payment until Víctor has found a job, which he hasn't. It seems the last thing this small town needs is another lawyer.

This might turn out to be a blessing in disguise. A few nights ago, Víctor admitted to his daughters (and this is a family secret, so it'd be great if it were kept between the covers of this book) that for a long time now, he has not been happy practicing law. Too much arguing. Too many people in trouble.

But what could he do instead?

Papa isn't sure. Growing up poor, he had to work to help out his family and put himself through school. He used to dream of playing baseball, or at the very least, coaching it. But he has already contacted all the local schools, and everyone is set with their sports staff for the year. "I'll find something, don't worry," he has assured his daughters. "Maybe a job where I can make people happy for a change. And hey, guess what? I've already got the best job of all, being your father." Too bad that being a parent is not a paying job.

Victoria is looking around the room. "Any more ideas?" Five kids, an intelligent dog, a magical *tía,* surely they can come up with one moneymaking scheme!

Juanita has been wondering what she can do that someone might pay her for. Suddenly it occurs to her. "Remember how everyone this last summer loved my flowers and kept saying they wanted me to come over and help out in their garden?" Tía Lola nods energetically, which sort of makes up for the fact that no one else remembers this compliment. "I can sign up people to help them with their flowers!"

She is so excited that even her know-it-all brother doesn't have the heart to remind her that it is mid-September. Vermont is headed for winter. The Swords *will* starve if they have to wait for grocery money until gardening weather in April.

Victoria wishes she could offer babysitting, but Papa has refused even to discuss the idea until Victoria turns thirteen, which won't be until next February. And that's just *discussing* the idea, not *letting* her do it. Meanwhile, Papa is perfectly okay with letting Victoria babysit her sisters without paying her for it.

"I could cook and clean people's houses and take in sewing and ironing." Tía Lola is rattling off everything and anything she can think of to do. "And I could give Spanish lessons, cooking lessons, dance lessons—"

"Oh, oh, oh!" Cari is waving her hand. She has just started kindergarten, where raising your hand is such a big rule that now she raises her hand even at home. "I can give ballet lessons!" She is so proud of herself for thinking of something to keep her family from starving.

"You can't teach ballet! You're only five years old." Essie would have to be the naysayer.

But Cari is already on her toes doing a pirouette to prove she can so teach ballet. Everyone claps. "I can also teach handstands!" She tries one, but overdoes the swing of her legs and flops over on the floor. Who cares? It's the effort that counts. Everyone claps again.

Everyone but Essie, who rolls her eyes. But before she can naysay handstand lessons, Essie is stopped by a look from her older sister. It's one of those if-looks-could-kill looks that Victoria is so good at. Maybe her older sister should hire herself out as a hit man. No fingerprints, no smoking gun. Just a glance. She'd be in high demand. No one would suspect the sweet, responsible Victoria of being a killer.

But Victoria isn't feeling particularly sweet or responsible. She glances down at her list. Except for Tía Lola's offers, the rest are ridiculous! Baseball tutoring? Sword fighting? Handstand and ballet lessons given by a five-year-old? It takes all of Victoria's self-control not to bunch up her sheet of paper and toss it into the trash can.

●●●

As they ride their bikes home from town, Tía Lola and Miguel and Juanita are quiet. Each one is still preoccupied with how to help the Espada family.

At the corner of their road stands the two-story house where Papi and Carmen have sometimes stayed on weekend visits. Tía Lola stops, head cocked, reading the sign: BRIDGEPORT B&B

"Miguel and Juanita, I always forget to ask when we pass this place. Why don't the owners finish the sign?"

"Finish it, Tía Lola?" Miguel doesn't understand. It's the same old, weathered sign that's been up since before they moved to this road.

"Aren't the owners going to spell out their names?"

Miguel smiles, amused. Tía Lola arrived in the United States only last year, and sometimes she doesn't understand how things work here. "A B&B is the name of a kind of hotel in someone's house, like staying with a friend, but you have to pay for it."

"That's a shame," Tía Lola says, shaking her head in disapproval. "To charge your friends."

"But they're not really your friends," Juanita adds. "It's just a way for a family to earn some money. Using their own house as a hotel."

A look has come over Tía Lola's face that Miguel and Juanita know well. The opposite of a if-looks-could-kill look; it is a if-looks-could-save-the-world look. The beauty mark on her forehead glows like a bright star. Some fun and fantastic idea is brewing in their aunt's head. Before they can stop her, Tía Lola has turned her bicycle around and is pedaling back to town. "Hey, Tía Lola! It's this way to our house!"

But Tía Lola can't hear them. By now she is a distant blur. And all Juanita and Miguel can do is turn their bikes around and try to catch up with her.

● ● ●

"I have a solution!" Tía Lola has burst into the room where Colonel Charlebois and the Espada girls have just sat down to tea. Miguel and Juanita trail in behind her. All three are out of breath after their fast and furious bike ride into town.

"What on earth are you talking about?" Colonel Charlebois exclaims once he has settled Tía Lola in a chair. "A solution to what?"

"Oh, just a family project," Victoria says vaguely. She casts a warning look over at Essie and Juanita, the two blabbermouths. If they confess to the colonel that Papa doesn't want to be a lawyer anymore and can't find any other job, the colonel is liable to throw the Espadas out of the house. No, wait; that's not what the kind old man would do. He'd probably try to give them charity, which Papa would never accept. Victoria doesn't get why her father has to be so against charity. After all, he named his own baby girl Caridad, which means "charity" in Spanish.

The colonel rises from his chair. "If you'd like to have this conversation in private . . ."

"No, *coronel, por favor,* you must stay." Tía Lola has finally caught her breath. Her heart has settled down. "This solution will require your permission and participation."

Now it's the colonel's heart doing a little skip and jump. Not since his army days traveling all over the world has he felt this stirring of excitement. There's life in the old man yet! He sits back down in his chair, eyes gleaming. "Go on."

First things first. "What does a B&B stand for?" Tía Lola asks.

"A bed-and-breakfast," the colonel says without hesitation. "Guests pay for a bed and their breakfast."

"And how much does this guest pay for this bed and this breakfast?"

"Oh, I don't know. I'm not in the market for a B&B, so I've not kept up with prices. Why are you asking, if I may ask?"

"*Bueno, coronel,* you may soon be in the market for a B&B, so if you would be so kind as to find out what it costs, we—"

"You mean you're throwing me out of my own house?" the colonel cuts her off gruffly. He has a look of alarm on his face, but there is a twinkle in his eye.

"*Ay, coronel,* where are my manners?" Tía Lola has forgotten to ask first if the colonel would entertain her moneymaking solution. "Remember how you said you prefer living with company?"

"Well, yes. But I've got very fine company here now." He nods at the three Espada girls, who are all looking quite perplexed.

"But they are your renters, and I am speaking of guests."

"Guests, you say?" The colonel scowls, but even the Espada girls, who have known him only a couple of months, can tell he is intrigued. "But where will we put them?"

"Here is my proposal."

They all pull their chairs around the tea table as Tía Lola draws a ground plan of Colonel Charlebois's house. On the first floor, the colonel can keep his bedroom. But if the Espadas move one floor up to the little attic rooms, that would free up three bedrooms on the second floor for B&B guests. "What do you think, *coronel?*"

Everyone turns expectantly to the old man. The Espada girls are ready to throw themselves at his feet and beg him to please, please, please let them run a B&B out of his house.

This could be sooooo exciting, Victoria is thinking. Maybe a family with teenage boys will stay here. Papa has absolutely ruled out even talking about dating until Victoria is in high school. But if boys are guests, Victoria can hang out with them and not have to disobey her father.

Maybe a famous baseball player will come to their B&B and befriend the amazing athlete Esperanza Espada. Essie's heart soars. She can already see herself at Fenway Park, a guest of the Red Sox, sitting in their dugout.

Cari doesn't care who comes, just as long as it's not someone scary. But then she remembers Colonel Charlebois is a hero with medals for his bravery. He would defend her. And there's always Valentino.

Although this B&B won't be in their house, Miguel and Juanita are excited, too. First of all, anything Tía Lola thinks up is sure to be fun. Second, winter is coming, that boring time of year when you can't go outside and play baseball or grow flowers. It'll be good to have a fun project in town.

Colonel Charlebois takes a big breath, as if he were about to blow out all eighty-five candles that will be on his birthday cake this December. "I think it's a terrific idea!"

A cheer goes up. High-fiving all around.

"I guess Papa does have to vote." Victoria is nothing if not fair.

"Well, that's the end of that solution," Essie says in a gloomy voice. "You know Papa, and how he doesn't want to impose on Colonel Charlebois."

"This is my house!" Colonel Charlebois reminds her. "I can do what I want here."

"Try telling that to Papa." Victoria sighs. Valentino, who understands the language of sighs, comes over and licks her hand.

It's as if a glove has been flung in challenge at the old soldier. "I *will* tell him. If I want to turn my house into Tía Lola's B&B, you better believe I will, no matter what Víctor Espada has to say about it!"

They're all back on their feet again, high-fiving and cheering. Which is why no one hears the front door open or the footsteps coming down the hall toward the room where there's quite a commotion going on.

Papa is at the door, arms folded, looking disapprovingly at his daughters. "Girls, you need to keep your voices down. This is Colonel Charlebois's house." For some reason, his reminder brings on a renewed round of loud laughter.

"Would someone care to tell me what is going on?" Papa asks sternly.

The children all raise their hands.

But Colonel Charlebois pulls rank. "I'll do the explaining here," he says. "After all, this *is* my house."

TíA LOLA stories

Read them all!

Now available in Spanish!
¡Ahora disponible en español!

Meet Tía Lola, an Aunt like No Other

How **Tía Lola** Came to ~~Visit~~ Stay

Moving to Vermont after his parents split, Miguel has plenty to worry about! Tía Lola, his quirky, *carismática,* and maybe magical aunt makes life even more unpredictable when she arrives from the Dominican Republic to help out his Mami.

"*Simple, bella, un regalo permanente:* simple and beautiful, a gift that will stay."　　　　　　　　—*Kirkus Reviews*

★ "The warmth of the individual characters and the simple music of the narrative will appeal to middle-graders. So will the play with language." —*Booklist,* Starred

Go Back to School with Tía Lola!

How **Tía Lola** Learned to Teach

Tía Lola has been invited to teach Spanish at her niece and nephew's elementary school. Juanita can't wait to introduce her colorfully dressed aunt to all her friends at school. But Miguel isn't so sure. . . .

"A welcome return for a wonderful character whose heart encompasses the whole world." —*School Library Journal*

"Alvarez invites everybody—no matter their background—into this welcoming family and community."
—*The Horn Book Magazine*

Welcome to Summer Camp—Tía Lola-Style

How **Tía Lola** Saved the Summer

When the Guzman household is invaded by houseguests, Miguel thinks his vacation is ruined. But Tía Lola has a few tricks up her sleeve to make this the best summer ever!

"Tía Lola is that special aunt who knows how to add a touch of fun to everything!"   —TimeforKids.com

"Replete with adventure and humor. . . . Returning readers will rejoice in reconnecting with the effervescent Tía Lola and the rest of the gang, while even readers new to the tales will want to read more about Vermont's favorite Dominican aunt."   —*Kirkus Reviews*

Tía Lola's Bed-and-Breakfast: Now Open for Business

How **Tía Lola** Ended Up Starting Over

Tía Lola and the children are opening their own bed-and-breakfast. But they soon realize that running a B&B isn't as easy as they thought—especially when someone is out to sabotage them! Who is causing these mysterious mishaps? Tía Lola is on the case!

Like all the Tía Lola Stories, this fourth and final installment comes with plenty of heart and a surprise at the end!

"A fitting farewell to a memorable character."

—*Kirkus Reviews*

YEARLING HUMOR!

Looking for more funny books to read?
Check these out!

- ☐ *Bad Girls* by Jacqueline Wilson
- ☐ *Calvin Coconut: Trouble Magnet* by Graham Salisbury
- ☐ *Don't Make Me Smile* by Barbara Park
- ☐ *Fern Verdant and the Silver Rose* by Diana Leszczynski
- ☐ *Funny Frank* by Dick King-Smith
- ☐ *Gooney Bird Greene* by Lois Lowry
- ☐ *How Tía Lola Came to ~~Visit~~ Stay* by Julia Alvarez
- ☐ *How to Save Your Tail* by Mary Hanson
- ☐ *I Was a Third Grade Science Project* by Mary Jane Auch

- ☐ *Jelly Belly* by Robert Kimmel Smith
- ☐ *Lawn Boy* by Gary Paulsen
- ☐ *Nim's Island* by Wendy Orr
- ☐ *Out of Patience* by Brian Meehl
- ☐ Shredderman: *Secret Identity* by Wendelin Van Draanen
- ☐ *Toad Rage* by Morris Gleitzman
- ☐ *A Traitor Among the Boys* by Phyllis Reynolds Naylor

Easton Public Library

Visit **www.randomhouse.com/kids** for additional reading suggestions in fantasy, adventure, mystery, and nonfiction!